BLACK FLAME

Gerelchimeg Blackcrane

Translated by Anna Holmwood

Groundwood Books / House of Anansi Press
Toronto Berkeley

Groundwood Books / House of Anansi Press
110 Spadina Avenue, Suite 801, Toronto, Ontario M5V 2K4
or c/o Publishers Group West
1700 Fourth Street, Berkeley, CA 94710

We acknowledge for their financial support of our publishing program the
Government of Canada through the Canada Book Fund (CBF).

Library and Archives Canada Cataloguing in Publication
Blackcrane, Gerelchimeg
Black flame / written by Gerelchimeg Blackcrane ; translated
by Anna Holmwood.
Translation of: Hei yan.
Also issued in electronic format.
ISBN 978-1-55498-135-9 (bound).—ISBN 978-1-55498-107-6 (pbk.)
1. Tibetan mastiff—Juvenile fiction. I. Holmwood, Anna II. Title.
PZ7.B5315Bl 2013   j895.1'36   C2012-905755-X

Cover illustration by Harvey Chan
Design by Michael Solomon
Groundwood Books is committed to protecting our natural environment.
As part of our efforts, the interior of this book is printed on paper that
contains 100% post-consumer recycled fibers, is acid-free and is processed
chlorine-free.
Printed and bound in Canada

CONTENTS

1

A SNOWY NIGHT

IT WAS SNOWING for the second time that spring. The large, heavy flakes gathered high up in the sky before falling for as far as the eye could see, each flake trying to deprive the earth of its first smatterings of green. After nightfall, the snow fell more quickly, smothering the land in its embrace — rustling, whistling, hustling and jostling — almost instantly blotting out the remains of the last snow yet to melt on the ground. The snow became heavier, forming thick layers across the sky, until eventually not even the slightest chink or crevice remained.

This was the northern Tibetan plateau, the place they call the world's third pole, sitting at the very top of a world of ice. It made you think of the very beginnings of the universe. It was wild, far from human civilization and bleak.

Yurts are like tiny islands in the plateau's brutal snowstorms. As insignificant as licks of fire in the vast wilderness, they seem in danger of being swallowed up by snowdrifts at any moment. A herdsman can construct a yurt in a matter of minutes, instantly creating a warm home against the wind and snow, one that he can always take with him as he moves from place to place.

Mother Mastiff circled the yurt. Through the yak-hair walls, she could hear the faintest sound of a child crying and the gentle hum of its mother singing. Everything was as usual.

She walked behind the yurt to where the livestock were kept. A dozen or so yaks were being enveloped by the snow, forming white hillocks as they brought up and chewed once more on the grass that had been so difficult to find during the day. Their chewing sounded like wind blowing through lush autumn grass. As always, the sheep pressed together against the cold.

This was a new campsite. A month before, the master, Tenzin, had driven his livestock from their winter pasture to this location for the spring. The sheep and yaks were thin and exhausted after the harsh winter, but could now recuperate for a while and give their bodies a chance to fill out.

Mother Mastiff looked over and saw a slight smile of recognition spread across Tenzin's face, bright crimson from the violent plateau sun. She knew this expression well — it meant that he was in a good mood. At times like this, he might even spring toward her and pat her affectionately on the head. The ruthless days of winter were finally over. It was a May night up on the northern

Tibetan plateau, and all was as it should be, calm and quiet.

After surveying her territory, Mother Mastiff went to a pile of sheep's fleeces behind the yurt. She stretched out her paw and carefully moved one of the fleeces aside, and at once there was the sound of puppies whimpering. The three plump puppies smelled their mother and climbed out in search of her, their heads bobbing. A deep mastiff growl came from her throat, and she shook the heavy wet flakes from her body before lying down among the fleeces. The puppies impatiently burrowed their way under her belly, jostling for a teat in her long, thick fur. Once they found one, they held it tightly with their delicate paws and sucked greedily.

Mother Mastiff poked her head outside once more. It was so quiet. There was probably no need to look. Perhaps she was being unnecessarily cautious, yet a Tibetan shepherd dog never lets down its guard.

The puppies were almost a month old, and their mother knew that before long the master would take them and give them to herdsmen in pastures far away, just as he had done before. But she wasn't sad. The puppies already had teeth and were biting her nipples as they sucked at her decreasing supply of milk. Mostly, she bore their audacious biting in silence, but when it hurt too much, she would let out a low, muffled howl and gently shift her body.

The three purebred Tibetan mastiff pups were already as round as little balls, covered in thick fuzz the color of a crow's wings, a metallic blue shining through the lacquer black. Their veins were charged with noble blood, and they had a fearless hunger for life that the oxygen-starved plateau bestowed on all the animals who lived upon it.

The night got darker, and the snow grew heavier. Despite the snow's attempts to swallow every sound, there were still some noises coming from the livestock, noises that alarmed Mother Mastiff. She raised her heavy head, but her moist nose couldn't detect any of the signs of danger that usually accompanied these sounds. She couldn't see anything, and the air was still. And yet the sounds of a disturbance continued to reach her, sounds that she shouldn't be hearing on such a peaceful snowy night.

Something was going on.

She stood up, but the puppy with the largest head who always had the teat with the most milk couldn't bring himself to let go. He hung from his mother's belly, clinging to her nipple. The desperate cry of one sheep in particular floated up from the flock, and she could hear the muffled sound of the yaks stomping their hooves fretfully on the loosely packed snow. She had ignored these sounds for too long.

Mother Mastiff shook her body. The puppy finally fell from her nipple, rolling on the ground and crying out at having lost such a delicious teat. Mother Mastiff pushed him back under the fleeces with her nose before stepping out into the soft snow, which now reached halfway up her legs. She ran through the dark to the sheep.

As she ran, she barked a warning to the master in his yurt in that deep steady way that is special to Tibetan mastiffs. It sounded like a stone striking a drum of stretched cow leather.

By the time she reached the flock, all the yaks were standing, their fur frozen in clumps of snow and ice like suits of armor. They looked like large drifting rocks. The sheep were pressed together tightly into one mass.

A strange smell. Mother Mastiff instantly distinguished a smell richer than that of sheep and from the wilds. A smell as powerful as that of the fear emanating from the sheep. It was coming from the center of the flock.

Howling in fury, she crashed with all her might into a sheep on the edge of the flock, but despite being hit hard in the stomach, the sheep maintained a look of indifference. It kept absolutely still, only narrowing its expressionless eyes, its frost-encrusted lashes fluttering like a startled butterfly's wings. Sheep are like that. As soon as anything happens, their only response is to draw together tightly. Mother Mastiff tried again several times, but the sheep didn't react. There was nothing she could do, so she ran around them, barking wildly, trying to find an opening that would allow her to find the sly good-for-nothing hiding in the middle.

She made herself hoarse barking in the direction of the yurt for Master to hurry outside. She had no means of penetrating the flock, and anger enflamed her. Her ferocious nature was urging her to find the scoundrel who was no doubt tucked under the belly of a sheep, secretly laughing at her. She would rip it into tiny pieces. She charged at the trembling flock, whose bleats sounded like muffled thunder. She knew that whatever was hiding in among those sheep couldn't stay there forever.

Just as she predicted, it emerged.

But she didn't foresee the lightning-quick attack that followed. All she heard was something screaming toward her, and then she felt a heavy blow to her right side that nearly knocked her to the ground. She shifted her feet and found her center of gravity, her considerable size still giving her the advantage.

The ghostly shadow stopped on the snow in front of her. It was a snow leopard. Mother Mastiff's bark had interrupted its dinner. It was a resplendent piece of satin against the snow, its tail as thick and strong as a python dragging behind its body. The leopard stared casually at its opponent. Its attack on the sheep had been an easy victory, and it opened its large mouth, still smeared with fresh red blood, and let out a roar like cracking ice.

The muscles in Mother Mastiff's shoulder had been ripped open, and warm blood was seeping into her long fur. The smell of blood only made her angrier. But she also relaxed. The physical presence of the snow leopard was more reassuring than a hidden opponent. Slowly, she began to rock her head, her eyes fixed on the cat in front of her.

A Tibetan mastiff's vocabulary contains no word for

fear. Purebreds are simply not afraid of predatory animals. Yet in all her time protecting Master's campsite and his livestock, Mother Mastiff had never fought a snow leopard.

The 130-pound mastiff and the snow leopard faced each other in perfect silence. The only sound was of snow falling to the ground. The sheep were now huddled into an even more compact mass, as if they could only convince themselves that they were safe by pressing together so tightly.

Without a sound, Mother Mastiff flew forward. Once again, the snow leopard made an unexpected move. Instead of relying on its quick reactions to dodge her, it chose to meet her attack. And just as the mastiff sank her teeth into the leopard's shoulder — with its scent of snowy mountain peaks — the leopard's paw lodged itself into her back like a steel hook.

She pulled away decisively, and with a roar, she went to bite the paw that had punctured her skin and was now digging its way even deeper into her flesh. Her teeth met the leopard's sharper teeth, which were still covered in sheep's blood, their clash giving off a sound like clinking metal.

After this encounter, Mother Mastiff felt only a throbbing in her back. She hadn't been injured elsewhere. The leopard, who had given its all, stood a short distance away in the trampled snow. The mastiff slowly edged closer as the leopard roared with all its might, revealing a weakness in spite of its fearsome appearance. It was trying desperately to hide one of its front legs, which had been badly hurt. Although Mother Mastiff hadn't heard the crisp sound of bone snapping when she bit the leopard's paw, she was still savoring the satisfaction of having severed firm muscle and tendon.

It had stopped snowing. Almost at once, the navy blue sky filled with stars, and the snowy ground dazzled in the moonlight as the last flakes reluctantly fell from the sky, searching for a place to settle.

Having lost the cover of darkness, the fully grown snow leopard was clearly worried. The hair on its tail stood erect and thicker than usual, swaying gently like a snake charmed by a flute, as if animated by some secret intent. The leopard had already used the time the two animals stood looking at each other to scan the way it had come.

Mother Mastiff knew that if the snow leopard hadn't been hungry, it would have left long ago. In such nasty weather, there was no guarantee of finding food every day, so it would be reluctant to leave behind the meat it had already secured.

As she lunged forward, Mother Mastiff knew that this would be her final attack — she was using up the last of her energy. She was confident that she could dodge the paw that was coming her way and then sink her teeth into the leopard's throat before pressing it to the ground, where she would wait for its warm blood to run out onto the snow. Then she would hear a hollow trickling, like the sound of her mistress collecting water from the river with her wooden ladle. Once she opened her mouth, the leopard's head would slide softly onto the snowy ground, just like those of the two greedy wolves she had defeated only recently.

She charged at the hesitant snow leopard and pretended to bite its injured right leg. Fooled, the leopard's instant reaction was to lower its head to fend her off. Everything was going according to plan. Experience is important in these things, and she had gathered a lot of it defeating the wild animals that had threatened their campsites over the years.

Suddenly she heard the sound of chirping, as if from a small startled bird. Propelled by a mother's instinct, she looked over toward the fleeces, now blanketed in snow. But by the time she realized that this was a mistake, it was too late. Taking advantage of Mother Mastiff's temporary distraction, the snow leopard quickly sank its sharp teeth into her exposed belly.

What followed was as chaotic and unfathomable as a nightmare. The roaring was terrifying. It sounded as if things were crashing and rolling around on the snow close to the yurt. Tenzin was dazed, having spent the night suffering from a high fever, and only when everything became quiet again did he seem to stir from his coma-like stupor.

He eventually climbed out from under the blanket, and ignoring his wife's protests, tottered out into the yard. In his right hand, he carried a long Tibetan sword and in his left, a flashlight. The clouds had disappeared, and the sky was an emerald blue. Moonlight illuminated the snow. Everything was quiet, as if nothing had happened. Too quiet. Only the sheep huddled tightly together instead of lying on the ground suggested that everything was not as it should be.

Tenzin noticed that for some ten yards around the sheep the snow had been trampled, revealing the grass beneath, and the snow that remained was dotted with spots of congealed blood. Something that looked like a soft plush blanket had been tossed on the ground. Still gripping the sword in one hand and the flashlight in the other, he walked toward the bloodstained bedding. He edged closer and nearly dropped his flashlight in astonishment.

It was a snow leopard. It had a shocking rip in its throat, revealing startlingly red muscles and a confusion of veins and windpipes. Its round eyes were still open. Holding the sword tightly, he drew the blade across the leopard's chest, but it didn't move. It was dead. Its magnificent coat was decorated with spots of blood, and it was so beautiful it made him tremble.

A broken trail of blood led to the pile of sheep's fleeces behind the yurt. Tenzin was shaken by the scene that greeted him. The blood that had poured from Mother Mastiff's wounded belly had already stained a large patch of snow. She heard him and sluggishly tried to raise her head before nudging one of the puppies who had been pushed aside back to her chest. The three puppies were sucking at their mother's nipples, seemingly unaware of what had happened.

The moonlight disappeared. It was now the darkest part of night, just before dusk. Mother Mastiff suddenly looked up from where she lay in a corner of the yurt. Confused, she sniffed at the butter-soaked rag tied around her middle before discovering, to her relief, that Master had carried her puppies inside and placed them on a sheep's fleece nearby. She carefully licked the blood from their coal-black fur, and they merely groaned a few times in their sleep. They must have had their fill of milk.

Once she had licked them clean, she wobbled to her feet like a prayer flag flapping in the wind and then steadied herself. She leaned down to sniff the puppies and then stumbled toward the felt rug hanging over the doorway. Pushing it aside with her head, she slipped out.

Tenzin didn't stop her. The first mastiff he had ever raised had left like this when he realized that the fire of his life was about to go out. All Tibetan mastiffs leave calmly when they know they are going to die. As long as they have the choice, they won't die in their campsite.

Tenzin pulled the rug aside and looked out at the translucent snow. Mother Mastiff was walking toward the vast mountains in the distance — blue brushstrokes already bathed in the first light of morning. By the time her dark shadow had disappeared beyond the horizon, the sun was up.

2
BLACK FLAME

KELSANG'S FIRST MEMORY was of a brilliant white snow-clad peak, set against a vast expanse of azure sky. The crystalline summit glistened in the sunlight, piercing his young eyes. Reluctantly, he lowered his head and licked the milk that had already begun to freeze in his steel bowl.

He was a fine example of a Tibetan mastiff. Heart-shaped ears hung on either side of his head, and now that he had lost his puppy fur, his coat was a crow-colored black with flecks of metallic blue. Even though he was only three or four months old, he was already showing signs of what was sure to become a frighteningly large frame.

Despite the difficulty of communication across the northern plateau, word spread in only a couple of weeks of the mother mastiff whose strength had equaled that of a snow leopard. A number of herdsmen spent days driving their horses across the grasslands in the hope of acquiring one of her offspring. They sincerely believed that such ferocity and courage were passed down through the blood.

Kelsang had few memories of his mother, and of the two siblings who had been carried away by the visiting herdsmen. He couldn't know that his master, Tenzin, had kept him because in just two short months his four paws had grown to be as big as a child's fists. He was an unfinished giant. Tenzin knew that he would grow so big that people would stare at him in amazement. Such a mastiff was necessary in a camp on the Tibetan plateau. He would protect the livestock, guard the yurt and even deliver messages when the camp was shut in by snow.

"Kelsang!"

The little dog heard his master's shout as he chewed on a piece of sheep shoulder. Although he wasn't sure that this was his name, every time Master made this sound he stared at him expectantly. And whenever Kelsang responded by trotting over, Master would do something that he found pleasing, like softly stroking his fur or fishing out a piece of dried meat from his sheepskin robe to give to him. As he chewed on the deliciously flaky meat, which had been left to hang in the dark all winter, his master would crouch down beside him and gaze out at the flock in front of the yurt.

But this kind of affection didn't happen every day, and aside from the extra ladle of milk his mistress gave him after she'd finished milking, he wasn't spoiled. Still, he didn't feel hard done by. He had mastiff blood in his veins, and mastiffs are not accustomed to having intimate contact with humans.

After the other two puppies were taken away, Kelsang was sent out of the yurt. The first night, he stubbornly paced in front of it, wailing to go back to the warmth inside. Suddenly Master pulled back the rug and struck him on the head with his *baiga*, a weapon made of a leather strap and pouch in which the herder places a stone or small pellets. Kelsang shrieked in pain and escaped in the direction of the livestock in an attempt to find some warmth among them.

The yaks began to stamp their excrement-encrusted hooves before he could get close. The sheep, in contrast, huddled together silently, their eyes shining in the dark like a galaxy reflected in a lake. Kelsang had no way of penetrating the flock and becoming one of them. He turned and went back to the yurt. A chink of warm light shone through a crack in the doorway, and he could hear the sound of Master's cheerful laughter. The young mastiff tried wailing again, but Tenzin replied with an angry shout, and so Kelsang went away, not wanting to suffer another blow to the head.

He nuzzled into the pile of sheep's fleeces, drinking in their familiar fragrance. He recalled the night his mother had been attacked by the snow leopard, and trying to suppress his fear, he started howling again.

From now on, he would no longer think of the warm fleece by the fire in the yurt. Far in the distance, a snowy peak radiated unnerving rays of silver moonlight like a rare jewel. Still howling, he wriggled deeper into the fleeces to escape the cold and then drifted off to sleep, enveloped by the smell of fresh grass.

Early morning on the plateau. The night's frost melted in the rays of the rising sun, turning into sparkling dew, like discarded pearls. Kelsang crawled out of the fleeces, crushing the pearls with each step as he scuttled toward the yurt.

A few dozen sheep had been tied horn to horn with a leather cord and were standing silently in front of the yurt, a drowsy look in their eyes, their udders swollen with milk as they waited for the mistress to milk them. Those who couldn't wait until after they'd been milked stuck their tails up in the air and discharged clusters of oily black excrement.

In the distance, a mass of gray clouds was being swept across the dark blue sky by the wind, leaving a shifting shadow as it flew over the grasslands. The shadow moved over the snowy peak like a tidal wave in retreat, and the sun's rays spread into every corner of the landscape. Master had already lit the mulberry embers in front of the yurt, and a curl of smoke was rising into the clear sky.

Kelsang sensed that something was different today. Usually Mistress would busy herself around the camp after giving him his milk, but today she and Master stood near him, whispering. Even though he could guess that whatever was about to happen had something to do with him, he was still a dog, and to him the most important thing was to gulp down the warm milk that had been placed before him. When his stomach rumbled, nothing else mattered, so he lowered his head and began slurping it up. By the time he had licked his way to the bottom of the bowl, Master had gone.

Just like every day that had come before this one, Kelsang had nothing to do after his meal other than to circle the yurt, then lie down near the pile of fleeces and stare blankly at the snowy peaks in the distance. He knew that soon Master's child would start gabbling, then scramble out of the yurt to play with him. But today the little boy followed Master around instead. Tenzin was carrying the fleece bag that he used for his lunch when he went out with the herd. When the child finally did run toward him, chattering merrily, Kelsang felt agitated. He stood up, preparing for a tussle, but Master barked a warning that sent the reluctant child off to one side.

Tenzin swung his *baiga* upward, and it let out a strong, crisp sound as it cut through the air. The flock of sheep in front of the yurt clambered to their feet. It was time to go out to pasture, just as they did every day.

"Kelsang!" Master called, turning around after walking a few steps.

Kelsang had been about to lunge at the child, but now he froze and without further hesitation followed his master. He didn't know why he did this, but he had a feeling that something was waiting for him. Every day, after strolling around the yurt in mind-numbing boredom, he would lie down on the grass and take a nap.

Deep within each pore he could feel a hunger growing, as if he were searching for something, but for what he couldn't be sure.

Carefully matching his master's pace, Kelsang walked with him into the grasslands. The wailing child had long since been pulled back into the yurt. Even though Kelsang was only a puppy, he suddenly realized that the days of playing with the child were over. He raised his large head, and relaxing his pace, followed his master, neither overtaking him nor falling behind. This was the beginning of his nomadic life, of moving in search of pasture.

As the black shadow of the yurt sank into the ashen horizon, Kelsang and his master finally reached a low-lying patch of lush grass. Master drove the sheep down into the depression, then leaned back against its slope, facing the sun. He took a clump of wool and a spindle, made from sheep thighbone, from the front of his robe and began to spin. The two hundred or so sheep spread out across the meadow and began their most important task of the day — eating.

Kelsang had never been this far away from the campsite before. The smell was completely different from the warm fragrance of burning dung that surrounded the yurt. It seemed that the brief but beautiful northern Tibetan summer had arrived. The sunlight was ample, the grass an exuberant green. Yet Kelsang still felt a tremble rise from deep within him. The grass beneath his feet was unfamiliar, the wind was blowing from a snow-capped mountain in the distance, and everywhere the air was full of the smell of the wilderness.

He lay down beside his master — the only place where he felt safe — and dozed, bathed in the sun's warmth. By the time he awoke, the sun had risen high in the sky, and Master had spun his thin strands of wool into thick thread, which he wound into a ball. Some of the sheep had taken a break from eating and were lying on the grass. The quiet was overwhelming, the sky a bright azure.

Suddenly a flash of gold started to make its way across the opposite slope. It was just the tiniest glint, but it was a vivid sight against the tranquil surroundings.

Kelsang launched forward, hearing his master's call but not yet used to obeying him unconditionally. He preferred to follow his own instincts, and he ran off, barking in pursuit.

But the small golden object suddenly disappeared. This was something Kelsang's young mind couldn't yet comprehend, and feeling confused, he slowed down. Whatever it was had left its trace, for a strange smell hung in the air. Kelsang's sense of smell was his most powerful tool for processing the world around him. This golden thing reminded him of the first time he had stepped out of the fleeces and seen the snow. A snowflake had fallen on his wet black nose, and within a moment it, too, had disappeared.

Kelsang carefully pressed his nose to the ground. He couldn't tell how far away it was, but the smell remained strong. Bit by bit, he was collecting and storing in his brain the many smells he encountered. This one was marmot, a rodent of the high plateau.

Following the smell, Kelsang came across a small hole in the ground. The scent was so strong, he felt as though it would swallow him whole. He was so excited that he nearly fainted — there was no doubt the creature was hiding in there. He dug away at the loose soil beside the hole. It wasn't that deep. He began to paw at the earth again when the marmot shot out through his legs, and before he knew what had happened, whizzed into the depths of the grasslands like a fat spinning top.

Kelsang ran after it, barking happily.

Maybe the marmot was a pioneer on these grasslands. It hadn't had enough time to dig a hole every ten yards or so, to pockmark the meadow so that when it was out hunting it had someplace to take refuge.

Marmots hadn't yet accumulated much fat by this time of year. This stubby little rodent was no real match for Kelsang, and after a while, it realized it was a mere plaything for the large dog. Kelsang knocked it over a few times with his paw but stopped short of killing it, even though he had many chances. Instead he let it get back up and run on.

Tenzin watched as Kelsang chased the marmot in circles. He wasn't going to stop him. He knew the only reason Kelsang was so engrossed in playing like this was because he was still young. He would soon learn how to guard the flock. It was in his blood.

Eventually, the marmot ran full circle back to its hole

and slipped in, sticking out its head, baring its teeth and letting out a squeal that sounded like a wild bird. Kelsang adjusted his pace as he ran toward it. Just as he was about to bite the marmot's nose, he jumped over its head, turned and began another attack. This was a game Kelsang would never tire of — every time his teeth were about to sink into the nape of the marmot's neck, he leapt overhead.

The marmot didn't know what to do. It had come to these grasslands to live a peaceful life. Unable to bear such bullying, it sprang out of the hole it had been trying to shrink back into.

Kelsang hadn't realized that his body seemed to be waiting for this moment. His blood raging, he instinctively jumped to his feet and bit hold of the fleshy marmot, twisting its legs with all his strength.

The marmot thrashed and struggled.

Although Kelsang had strong neck muscles, he was still only a puppy. His paws gripped the ground tightly, and his teeth now held just as tightly to the marmot's throat. Then he felt something break, and a warm liquid flowed down the marmot's glossy fur, trickling into his mouth. He snorted with pleasure as the marmot's wriggling body slowly went limp, until it stopped moving altogether.

Kelsang placed the marmot's plump little body in front of his master.

But Master simply patted him on the head, then took a piece of dried meat from his fleece bag and put it in

Kelsang's mouth. Kelsang lay down as Master took the knife tucked into his waistband and began carefully skinning the marmot. That afternoon, before they drove the sheep back to camp, Master took the marmot fur, which was already half-dried by the sun, and hung it from his waist.

As soon as they returned, Master's son ran out and tried to grab hold of Kelsang. But even though there was nothing else to play with on this bleak scrap of grassland, Kelsang ran away. He wasn't going to let Master's son grab hold of the fur on the back of his neck anymore. Those kinds of games no longer interested him.

The weather was unusually fine when Kelsang followed his master to put the sheep out to pasture for the third time. As soon as they found some good grass, Master took out his ball of wool and spindle. Kelsang lay down beside him. He began to feel dizzy as he watched the twirling spindle and closed his eyes.

All these first experiences were to become essential memories that would guide him in the future — when he next wanted to deal with a startled marmot who wouldn't come out of its hole, for example.

The marmot was behaving like any animal that finds itself trapped. Kelsang dug his head into the hole to catch the nasty little fellow, whose wrinkled features resembled a frightened cat. But it wasn't that simple. A pair of sharp fangs appeared before him, which he now knew didn't belong to a grasslands rodent. Panic swept

over him as he imagined something coming from behind, blocking the hole on top of him.

Darkness fell. The rays of light that had leaked into
the hole from behind him disappeared, and the wrinkled features of the marmot, baring its teeth and waving its paws, sank into darkness. The blackness flooded
everything like lake water. The thing that Kelsang most
feared had come to pass. He was suffocating in the hole.

Terrified, he strained his neck and barked furiously,
his muscles tightening and pressing against the walls.
He felt a knock on his head.

Kelsang woke up on his back, his paws in the air. A
cloud swept across the peaceful sky, making a huge, fast-
moving shadow over the grasslands. Master was spinning. He had not been trapped in the dark, musty hole
after all. Feeling almost hysterical with relief, he jumped
to his feet and began to rub his neck against Master's
boots in delight.

But Tenzin wasn't particularly interested in the dog's
affectionate behavior. His gaze was fixed on the movements of his flock down in the low-lying meadow. He
quickly swung his *baiga*, propelling a stone from its
pouch. But it landed yards away from the flock — they
had gone too far. The sheep kept their heads bowed low,
eating the fresh grass as they drifted still farther away
and began to round a small hillock, where they would
soon escape from Tenzin's view.

Tenzin sighed, about to fetch them back, when Kelsang shot out like a burning black meteor, barking as he

charged toward the sheep. It was only as he was flying down the hill that he himself realized what he was doing.

For the past few days, every time Kelsang woke from a deep sleep he could feel a mysterious impulse rising in him, like an ever-punctual, unchanging tide. He seemed to be searching for something. He wanted to bring something back to its proper place. This impulse plagued him, and he had no way of restraining or releasing it.

He had watched Master send out stones to warn sheep straying from the flock, or else walk out himself to drive them on to lusher pasture. If Kelsang had had an older mastiff to show him what to do, he would have understood more quickly. But he was just a puppy. How could his young brain know what to do simply by looking at what lay before him? Yet even without a guide, the shepherding instinct that thousands of years of mastiff blood had instilled in him propelled him forward. It was an instinct that couldn't be suppressed.

His first attempt turned out to be a failure. He ran through the flock of frightened sheep, scattering them far and wide. Only afterward did he turn back, running in wide circles to the left and right, barking as loudly as his young throat could. The sheep, unaccustomed to this circling tactic, were about to run all over the place again but quickly discovered that they were no match for this rough young dog. Kelsang even nibbled one straggling sheep in order to gather it in.

This was his first time, after all. He couldn't be expected to round them up flawlessly like an experienced sheepdog. The sheep, as was their way, acted like beads of spilled mercury, sliding here and there with no structure or reason. Kelsang spent twice as long gathering the flock as an experienced sheepdog would have done, but he managed it in the end.

When the young dog bounded up to his master, he was disappointed to find Tenzin sitting just as he had left him. This was Tibet's northern plateau. Mastiffs were born to herd sheep, just as sheep and yaks were born to provide milk, meat and hides. It was just as God had planned it. Tenzin had not been worried about Kelsang's hesitancy with the sheep. He knew that one day the dog's instincts would take over. This ability to accept everything as it came, and to do so calmly, was what enabled the people of the grasslands to hold on to life so stubbornly despite the harsh conditions.

A stony stillness came over Tenzin's face. As the sheep began to draw close to the hillock again, he made a "Shh!" sound to the dog at his feet, and Kelsang shot up like an arrow.

Once again, Kelsang gathered the sheep together and came back to lie at his master's feet. It already felt natural to him. The first time, he had been driven by instinct, but the second time, experience guided him. He lay down on the grass and looked out at the sheep in the distance. It felt as if he had been looking after this flock for a very, very long time. Without any kind of training, he had begun his life as a shepherd dog on the northern Tibetan plateau.

3

FARTHER AND FARTHER
AWAY TO PASTURE

IT HAD BEEN a perfectly ordinary day. As evening approached, Kelsang and his master gathered the sheep and brought them back to camp. Kelsang searched for a place where he could lie down to watch the smoke curling into the air from the roof of the yurt.

Dusk on the grasslands teems with life, especially in summer. In the distance, a herd of gazelles were climbing along a steep, bumpy ridge, their shadows flashing across the landscape like flapping wings. The grass was golden in the light of the sunset.

Every day repeated the one before, and Kelsang's first birthday passed before anyone realized it. During that year, the young mastiff followed his master's family to their winter pasture before returning to the same stretch of grasslands for the summer.

That spring he had killed his first wolf, an old animal

almost deranged with hunger. He hadn't wasted much energy killing it. The wolf was so weak it could barely move its head.

Kelsang was no longer struck by the uncontrollable trembling that had overcome him that first time — the kill came naturally to him now. He chased all the hunger-crazed wolves that came near with a calm focus, taking quick command and pushing them to the ground with ease. On one occasion, he even managed to fend off an attack by two wolves at once. Tenzin was surprised that a year-old mastiff was capable of such feats, and he rejoiced that he had chosen to keep this fine specimen from the litter.

Before the vehicle arrived, Kelsang's acute sense of hearing picked up a humming sound, like a bee colony on the move. A slight feeling of excitement welled up inside him, and he looked expectantly toward the horizon. Not two minutes later, a hump-backed shiny beetle of a jeep appeared, a piercing light glinting off its windows.

Cars would pass through from time to time, each one bringing strange and exciting smells. The campsite was a few miles from a single-lane road that was soon to be abandoned in favor of a new highway. Only a couple of vehicles at most would drive past each month, and of those, only a few ever came up to the camp, usually in search of water or other supplies. Kelsang would gallop toward the vehicle, his frightening bark forcing his master to restrain him. Today was no exception. As the jeep carefully pulled into the campsite, gleaming in the light of the setting sun, Kelsang charged forward, biting at the tires, the rubber squeaking between his teeth.

Two men staggered from the jeep, their legs numb with pins and needles. But they still hurried to greet the master warmly with the traditional *tashi delek*, as was the Tibetan custom. Their gaze lingered on the mountains, painted golden yellow in the setting sun, before they followed Tenzin into the yurt. The smell of butter tea was even more alluring after a day of jostling on a surface so rough it could hardly be called a road.

Kelsang had already lost interest in the two travelers, and he turned his attention back up to those same snow-capped mountains. They towered on the edge of the grasslands like sharpened knives, like molten gold shaped by the wind, lightly dusted in snow and then cut open, their highest peaks swaying in the rushing air and slicing through the golden clouds.

The wind blew down from the mountains, carrying with it a whiff of snow. Deep within it was another smell that seared Kelsang's nostrils like a hot needle, forcing him to bring his gaze back from the golden clouds fluttering atop the highest peak. As he stood up under the weight of his chains, he spotted a gray shadow resting in a shallow depression not far from the flock. What he saw confirmed what his sense of smell had already told him. It was a lone wolf trying to take advantage of the herdsman's nap time to find itself some food.

Kelsang barked and roared, trying to throw off the

chains fastened around his neck. Master emerged from the yurt, recognizing that this was no ordinary bark. Shielding his eyes from the last rays of sun, he looked out toward the sheep but didn't see the salt-and-pepper colored wolf pressed against the ground. Still, he undid the chains that were now stretched taut under the strain of Kelsang's pulling.

The wolf had overestimated its own abilities and was so convinced of its superior hiding skills that it refused to accept that the raging mastiff had spotted it. But it had not chosen its hiding place well, and being upwind from the yurt, Kelsang had easily picked up its scent. Only when he was just ten yards away did the wolf reluctantly cast a last glance at the beautifully plump lamb within its reach and make a dash for the depths of the grasslands.

In just a few bounds, Kelsang was sure he would succeed. The wolf had clearly not made a catch in a very long time. It looked like a small leaf blowing in the wind, its thin fur just barely covering the sharp outline of its rib cage. Before long, its tongue was drooping from its mouth, and it kept turning to look at Kelsang as he drew closer and closer.

Kelsang didn't let the wolf run out of Master's sight and came within three yards of it without much effort. He was perfecting his attack technique with each new chase. The wolf stumbled over a mound of earth that appeared to have been dug up by some small animal, only just managing to steady itself with a few broken steps.

But this cost it another couple of yards, and Kelsang's nose nearly brushed up against its tail.

Kelsang summoned all his energy to leap forward and bite the wolf's middle. The wolf was fooled and turned around to bite back, a last-ditch attempt in the face of a hopeless situation. But Kelsang's trick move had left the wolf's neck exposed, right under his nose. It was only natural for him to bite into it. He lifted the wolf, planted his own feet firmly on the ground and violently shook its neck.

From the outset, the creature's fate was sealed. After such a strenuous attempt at a getaway, the wolf's heart was ready to burst. It was unimaginably light, and as it sailed out of Kelsang's mouth, bubbles of dark blood flew from the gaping hole in its neck.

Kelsang watched as the wolf's legs twitched, then bit hold of its neck again and sauntered back to the yurt. He dropped the wolf at the door, where Master and the two strangers were waiting. Master stroked the top of his head and slipped a piece of dried meat into his mouth. Kelsang was in no hurry to swallow it, instead baring his bloodstained teeth as he chewed. He growled at the two strangers who were cowering behind Master. Tenzin scolded him quietly, then grabbed him by the neck, led him over to his wooden post and fastened his chains.

As darkness fell, the two strangers stepped out of the yurt to take a walk after their evening meal. They slowly approached Kelsang, who was lying in the grass, edging closer only when they saw that he was tied up.

The mastiff had a large square head, with a broad forehead, short muzzle and wide nose, and he had the most muscular neck they had ever seen. His thick tail spun behind his body, which was covered in a dense coat of fur so black that it shone blue in the evening light. The dog was strong — you could tell from the way he had flung the dead wolf on the ground like a piece of cloth.

The tall skinny man wanted a closer look, and ignoring his friend's warnings, he crept forward a few steps. The other man stood farther away where he felt safe, remembering how the dog had charged at the jeep when they drove into the campsite. He had attacked their tires like a shark closing in on its prey. The man had felt the solid tires clank as if they'd been struck by a piece of iron, and he'd only dared step out of the vehicle to greet the herdsman once Kelsang had been tied up. The dog had looked at him coldly as he deposited the shredded wolf and had shown no response to his master's caresses. That wolf had been no scarier than a chicken to this dog. There was no way the man would have come this close if he hadn't known that the dog was tied to the post, and that the post was dug firmly into the ground.

Of course, Kelsang couldn't have known that while he was fully focused on chasing the wolf, the two men and Master had been watching him. The tall skinny man had a pair of binoculars, and he saw the precision with which Kelsang aimed for the wolf's main neck artery, rupturing it with just one bite. He saw the tiniest threads of bright red blood pump from the wound, slowing to a trickle like a drying spring. And yet the dog still didn't stop shaking the wolf. Only when he grew bored did he fling the animal to the ground like a lump of dough, its head almost completely severed from its body.

"Kelsang," he said to the dog lying on the ground. He had learned the mastiff's name from Tenzin. Kelsang looked up with an air of studied ignorance, an expression that said nothing bothered him. He was like a completely different dog from the one who had just ripped the wolf to pieces.

Perhaps the tall skinny man was deceived by Kelsang's feigned indifference. He had approached many dogs in the past, and usually after an attack like that they had no fighting instinct left. Or perhaps it was because his belly was full of the master's delicious food that he abandoned his usual caution and continued to edge closer.

Before he could take another step, a wall of black rose up in front of him. His friend called out in alarm. The tall skinny man scrambled out of reach like a trembling stick insect. He looked back at the giant dog, straining at his clanging chains. Kelsang's eyes were like two licks of fire flickering in his black fur, his gaze practically burning a hole in the man's flesh.

Kelsang spat out a piece of cloth and lay down again on his warm patch of grass. He didn't like the smell of that scrap of sleeve, but now he could add suntan lotion to his collection of known and recognized smells.

"You call that a dog? It's more like a lion!" the man said. He scrambled to his feet and began to brush the dirt and grass from his torn clothes. He was trying to draw attention away from his pallid cheeks, although, of course, it might have been the altitude that made him so pale, and not Kelsang's attack.

"They're scary dogs," said his companion, hugging himself as he retreated. "I've heard people say that a genuine mastiff from the plateau can kill three wolves at once, and maybe even a panther. Seems like they might be right."

"Of course they're right. These dogs survive where humans struggle. Two thousand years ago they spread to ancient Greece, then through the Roman Empire until they found themselves in Eastern Europe. Now all the world's most vicious dogs are descended from the Tibetan mastiff. He's grandfather to the grandfather of them all." The tall skinny man was grateful to have found a topic of conversation to show off his knowledge and to make his companion forget how fearful he'd been.

His friend decided that maybe he should read up on these dangerous breeds. Perhaps the look in the man's eyes made Kelsang uncomfortable, because he suddenly leapt to his feet and pulled at his chains. In the dusk light, he looked even more magnificent. The two men sighed in admiration and stepped farther away.

"I've got a friend in Chengdu who kept two purebred German shepherds to guard his house," said the tall skinny man. "But one night burglars tied them up and stole everything and then made off with the dogs as well. The dogs didn't make a sound when the burglars came in, so he ended up wasting over a thousand *yuan* a month on food alone. He asked me to help him find a purebred Tibetan mastiff — he's heard they're the only dogs that can really guard a house. Let's see if we can take this one back."

"What? Take this dog thousands of miles back to Chengdu?" Maybe the lack of oxygen had gone to his friend's head.

"Or we could take him to Lhasa and sell him at a specialist mastiff market. He'd fetch a ton," the tall skinny man said. He'd be able to buy a pick-up and start his gemstone business with the proceeds, he thought, growing more excited.

"But herdsmen don't tend to sell their dogs, do they?" the other man said, not wanting to dampen his friend's mood, but identifying a real problem.

"Nothing's impossible, especially up here on the plateau." The tall skinny man went to the trunk of the jeep and brought out two bottles. Then the two men slipped back into the warm glow of the yurt.

Kelsang leapt to his feet and pulled at his chains again, but to no avail. He sensed that something ominous was about to happen. The men's strange behavior was enough to make him sure of that.

The journey seemed very long.

Through the back window of the jeep, all that could be seen was the black outline of the yurt growing ever dimmer in the open stretch of landscape. Kelsang finally settled down after being extremely restless. But the strangeness of everything still frightened him. The stench of gasoline made him feel dizzy, and he felt nauseous from the scent of plastic and cigarette smoke that permeated the jeep's fittings. He had arrived in a world full of new smells.

The instant the outline of the yurt disappeared, an emptiness like he had never experienced before gripped Kelsang's fluttering heart. It felt like something had been whipped away from him. He thought he was a grown-up dog who could face anything bravely, but that feeling of security had vanished suddenly back at the camp, and now it was completely gone. He had no option but to lie back down and give himself time to think.

Early that morning, Kelsang had heard Master's footsteps, usually so firm and sure, stumbling out of the yurt. Master approached with a blank look on his face, the two strangers following him. There was something strange about the atmosphere of the camp, but Kelsang slowly stood up to greet his master, pretending nothing was wrong. Mistress and her son stood by the yurt's entrance watching. Master's eyes were glazed over, and he seemed to have no control over his steps, nearly falling on top of Kelsang.

A stink was coming from his body, a smell Kelsang had never encountered before. From then on, he would always remember the smell of alcohol because it marked such a dramatic change in his fate. The smell and Master's clumsy movements made him feel uncomfortable. Master seemed concerned that he hadn't tied him tightly enough. He had already fastened another chain around Kelsang's neck, and still not content, began to wrap more chains around his middle.

Kelsang shook his head with displeasure. Irritated, Master muttered something and boxed his left ear. The resentment and humiliation Kelsang felt were worse than the pain. He had never been hit like this before. Even when he was small and had done something wrong, the punishment had usually only been a warning.

He had no idea what was going on, but Master had tied him up so tightly that not even a panther could have escaped. Master then led him to the back of the jeep as the two strangers instructed, and locked him in. Then he stumbled to the yurt, unwilling to look back at Kelsang, bumping into his wife in his rush to get inside. Kelsang heard a dull thud as he fell to the ground.

Kelsang lay in the trunk grumbling because of the heavy metal chains pressing into his ribs. He had never been tied up like this. In the past, Master had only tied him up when strangers came, and he always removed the chains as soon as they left. He had had so many new experiences today. It was all so different from the blue skies, pastures and sheep that he was used to.

Kelsang stood up and looked out the back of the jeep. Now that their summer camp had completely disappeared, panic swept across his fragile heart like a cloud's shadow sweeping across the grasslands. He kept trying to tell himself that this was just one of Master's jokes, but that couldn't explain everything. He had never felt this frightened before.

The jeep spluttered up a gentle slope, and the meadows that gave Kelsang comfort were reduced to a stingy strip that bumped in and out of view from the window. The last thing that could console him had all but disappeared, and anger at being abandoned or kidnapped rose in his chest like a ball of fire. The jeep jolted over a small stone, and the tiny vibration set him off like a bomb.

The two men were shell-shocked by Kelsang's outburst. The man driving lost control of the steering wheel, and the jeep veered into a pothole, lurching rapidly to one side. Loose bottles and cans rolled and clanked into each other, the din heightening Kelsang's anxiety. Each bark was like a clap of thunder echoing in the jeep, and as he barked, Kelsang thrashed around hysterically, biting at whatever he could. In the open grasslands, his bark didn't have the power to shake people's souls, but in the confined space of the jeep, it was like setting off a fire-truck siren in a sealed room.

The jeep drove on for another thirty yards before coming to a stop. It was impossible to drive with a monster barking furiously in the back. Even with the utmost concentration, accidents were alarmingly common on these roads. The two men got out of the car, the color drained from their faces, and peered at the howling dog through the back window.

The fur on the back of Kelsang's neck was standing on end, and his eyes were burning. He looked like a lion whose food had been snatched away from him. He pounded blindly on the window like a well-oiled machine. Each strike sounded like the jeep's wheels hitting rock. The two men stared at Kelsang's infernal expression and his sharp white teeth magnified in the window. They didn't know what to do.

Kelsang's howling was no less chilling from outside the jeep. As soon as his perturbed whining found an outlet in the form of a half-open window, the sound gushed out like water breaking through a flood barrier. Every bark made the two men tremble as if ice water were being poured over their heads.

Kelsang crashed against the walls of his prison again and again, the confined space making him wild with fear. He was used to lying out in the open air or running wherever he pleased, even when winter temperatures on the plateau fell to minus forty degrees. But that life was a long way behind him now.

The jeep rocked back and forth with Kelsang's stubborn mechanical pounding. If he hadn't felt so helpless and been crashing all over the place rather than against one specific spot, the back door would have long since broken to pieces.

A smear of dark red appeared on the window where Kelsang had just hit his head, but the splashes of blood that followed didn't slow him down. The jeep continued to rock violently from side to side. The two men still didn't know what to do. The howling was starting to sear itself onto their brains. If they hadn't been so scared of being ripped to shreds, they would have set the crazed dog free by now. If he really was a dog, that is.

"I'll go mad if he keeps on." The tall skinny man's companion opened one of the jeep's doors, grabbed hold of a wrench and approached the trunk as if about to open it.

"Don't be stupid. You can't do that! This is no ordinary dog. You open that door and you'll be picking your own arm off the floor after he's ripped it clean off you!"

In fact, what happened was this. Emboldened by his weapon, the man walked around to the back of the jeep. But as soon as he saw Kelsang's face, twisted in anger, bashing against the toughened glass, he flinched and withdrew. Throwing down the wrench, he crumpled to the ground. Up at this altitude, people's reactions are slower than usual, and they often feel queasy. Keeping such a violent monster locked up was enough to make anyone crack. If the dog kept crashing against the jeep, he could smash through the window.

Finally, the tall skinny man came up with a plan, even though it would only give them temporary relief. The two men grabbed their camera bags and fled in the direction of a deep blue lake in the distance. Or rather they walked, because at this altitude strenuous movement was impossible. The monster left behind, locked inside the jeep, seemed to disappear. It turned out to be a good plan.

Down by the lake, they took photos of some rather ordinary birds in the water. But after an hour had passed, they had no choice but to go back. As they approached the jeep, it was eerily peaceful, almost as though it had been robbed.

"Maybe he had a heart attack," the tall skinny man's friend said, struggling with his camera bag, which he would have just slung over his shoulder at lower climes. His tone couldn't cover up the relief he felt.

"He's probably just resting." The tall skinny man sounded disappointed, even though he didn't mean to.

Steeling themselves, the two men peered through the window, which was now spotted with black bloodstains. The dog was neither dead nor resting, but crouched in a corner of the trunk as if ready to pounce. The red fireballs of his eyes were burning as brightly as ever. But he had finally stopped barking.

The jeep started to move again. Kelsang had experienced life's first defeat, and the pain in his shoulder spread like a fog through his entire body. Even though shepherd dogs on the grasslands are born with hearts as big as boulders and lungs to match, he was still gasping for breath, and he was getting more and more desperate for water. His throat was so dry, he could no longer growl in the way that made greedy wolves tremble. After being tossed and turned, his stomach felt like an enormous cavity, as hunger followed thirst. He longed for skimmed yak's milk, a drink he usually disdained, and his belly twitched uncontrollably at the thought of the creamy delicacy. But such fantasies only added to the pain of his predicament.

Endless jolting. Maybe the jeep was driving on a never-ending gravel beach. Kelsang stretched, stiffened his convulsing spine and threw up the remains of the meal he had eaten the day before. The *tsampa* barley flour had mixed with the ewe's milk in his stomach into a thick porridge. He felt much better afterward, and once the dizziness passed, his resilient body gained a new lease on life.

When night fell, the two men stopped at a simple guesthouse. They brought him a half-filled bucket of fresh water and a piece of roasted sheep's leg, just opening the jeep door wide enough to squeeze the bucket through while the tall skinny man held tightly to his chains. But the flames of Kelsang's anger had not been dampened by the monotonous journey. In fact, they now burned even brighter.

The water distracted him, otherwise he would have charged at the first person who dared let him out of the jeep and ripped them into tiny pieces. This thought was like a dormant volcano as the water doused his anger, delaying its eruption.

He leaned over the bucket and drank for a long time, until he was certain he had quenched his thirst. But as soon as the cold water reached his empty stomach, he felt hungry and had to put aside thoughts of venting his anger to concentrate on chewing the piece of mutton.

When he was finished, the tall skinny man approached carrying a forked stick and carefully opened the back door. Kelsang rushed at him, but the man was well prepared. He hooked the stick under the dog's leather collar so that no matter how hard he tried, Kelsang couldn't get at him.

In the meantime, the tall skinny man's friend undid one end of the chains and passed them to his companion. With the help of the stick, the tall skinny man led Kelsang to a wooden post in the middle of the courtyard and tied him up. Even though he was extremely careful not to let go of the stick wedged beneath the mastiff's jaw, Kelsang ran at him the moment he turned, nearly biting through his clothes.

The other guests had noticed the melancholy dog when the two men were feeding him, and the elaborate way they treated him only drew more attention. It wasn't every day that you could catch a glimpse of such a fine dog. As soon as Kelsang settled, they gathered around murmuring about how much he must weigh and the thickness of his limbs. Even though they knew nothing about Tibetan mastiffs, they could tell from his large frame that he was a rare specimen.

Kelsang, of course, didn't know that two years before his master had taken the entire family to the horse races, where Mother Mastiff met a pure black male from another part of the grasslands. Kelsang was the offspring of two of the finest mastiffs on the entire plateau.

The games started after the evening meal. All Kelsang wanted to do after eating was to lie down and relax. If he had been on the grasslands, his patrolling responsibilities would be done for the day, and he would be settling into a pile of sheep's fleeces. But he had already begun to sense that whatever was about to happen concerned him.

Two small bonfires were lit, using shards of wool, dried cow dung and the blue jet flames of a blowtorch, illuminating every corner of the courtyard. A dozen or so people began to crowd around — Kelsang had never seen so many. Their long shadows projected onto the guesthouse walls looked like giants emerging from deep underground.

Kelsang was nervous and ran around his wooden post twice, making raspy growling sounds from the depths of his throat. His fur was standing on end, and he looked unusually large in the firelight. It was still a glossy blue despite the thick covering of dust. He was like a floating ghost.

Everyone's eyes were fixed on him. It was obvious that something was about to happen, but he didn't know what. His gaze swept across the curious faces surrounding him. His eyes were like two bright rubies that shone from his black fur. The hair around his face stood as erect as an angry lion's mane.

He waited.

The crowd was fascinated by the huge mastiff, and gasps of admiration drifted into the night air. Someone was already trying to haggle over a price for him with the tall skinny man.

Kelsang barked, trying to break free from his chains. Two huge German shepherds were led into the yard, accompanying him with their howls. They were eager to get into the ring, but their collars were too tight, pulling the skin around their jaws and making the whites of their eyes sparkle.

Kelsang started to calm down, realizing that there was no point in pulling on his firmly fixed chains. Instead he turned his attention to the German shepherds. He had rarely encountered other dogs on the grasslands — the closest he had ever come were wolves. He began to compare them to the wolves he had met. Their ears were bigger, but their heads were not as wide. Their tails seemed to be more nimble, and their fur was a darker black.

"Two years ago I took a purebred German shepherd to the wilds and left her tied up to breed with wolves. She gave birth to these two — real wolfhounds. They could beat this mastiff any day." The army chef chose his words carefully.

Since Tibetan mastiffs were known as the kings of the canine world, no one raised any objection to the idea of having one dog fight two wolfhounds. The faces around Kelsang twinkled expectantly, but Master's was nowhere to be found.

Maybe they weren't wolves at all. They didn't smell of the wilds like the other wolves he'd met. No, their smell was even more familiar. It was the smell of the human world — of mutton and milk — left behind by owners after they stroked your fur. A wolf would never allow itself to smell of these things. So he could conclude that they weren't wolves. But he didn't have time to continue investigating. Their chains had been released, and the fat chef was encouraging them to go for him like pigs to the trough.

Kelsang calmly dodged the first dog's attack. His sharp teeth crunched together in midair as it flew past, his chains pulling tight and preventing him from getting close. He was just about to dodge the second dog, who was launching itself in the same fashion, when his chains pulled tight again, and he had to endure the full force of its attack. But Kelsang's fur was too thick for the dog's teeth to penetrate. The wolfhound was unable to slow its momentum and fell to the ground.

It was that simple. These dogs were much clumsier than the wolves on the grasslands. They didn't realize that this kind of powerful but clumsy attack left them vulnerable to their opponent's sharp teeth, and Kelsang wasn't about to give them a chance to correct their mistake. He jumped on the fallen hound's chest. It naively tried to bite his paw, but Kelsang had already ripped into its neck and was stalking away.

The speed at which all this took place clearly surprised the other hound, who was preparing to attack from behind. Crossbreeding usually results in smarter animals, with quicker judgment, but not with these dogs.

Gasps of fear — or perhaps admiration — rippled through the crowd. It only took seconds for the fat chef to realize how mismatched the fight was, and he began to shout in the hope that the other dog might turn back. But it was now crazy with anger at having lost its companion, barking like a puppy that has been struck by its master. It made straight for Kelsang.

Kelsang had already assessed the dog's strength, and rather than dodge it this time, he faced it head on. The fight was over so quickly, the spectators only heard the sound of teeth clashing and chains clanging before Kelsang had bitten through the dog's neck and tossed it aside. Even though the dog was dead, Kelsang still bit its main artery and blood drained onto the concrete.

The fat chef cursed loudly. It would take him at least a year to breed two more dogs, and even then he'd be lucky to have two as fine as these.

A couple of American backpackers seemed to recover from their shock and began chatting with the others. Two pieces of chocolate flew through the air and landed by Kelsang. He knew nothing of this strange food, but with the excitement of the massacre still coursing through his veins, he leapt toward it. Unfortunately, the chains held him back.

Kelsang watched as a man fetched a long iron rod and walked over to one of the dogs, who was still twitching on the ground. A loud shot. Kelsang jumped back fearfully, and the dog let out a last breath. It didn't take him long to understand what had happened.

Guns. In the days and months that followed, Kelsang would have more opportunities to become acquainted with these weapons that emitted such tremendous sounds and intense smells. He would always remember the unique scent of gunpowder and iron.

Now that he had vented the anger that had been building inside him all day, Kelsang felt unusually calm. He turned to lick the tiny cut on his left shoulder. The crowd dispersed, and the diesel generator roared into action, the guesthouse lights flickering on and off with the unreliable supply of electricity. The hubbub of voices rose and fell with the lights, everyone still caught up in the excitement of the fight.

Kelsang lay outside pondering the new life ahead of him. Once the bonfires were put out, the guesthouse became quiet. The full moon illuminated the vast expanse of grassland. Kelsang looked out at the road they had come along and could only imagine that this was the way back to his campsite, his old life. If he were there, he would be lying in a corner right now, looking out over the livestock and the snowy peaks clad in the steely light of the moon.

The middle of the night. Sounds of cattle chewing their cud and yaks clumsily knocking their hooves together. Everything that had once been so familiar was now edging farther away. Lying on the freezing concrete, Kelsang was doing what his ancestors had been doing for thousands of years — bearing the plateau's icy air with only his strong physique and long fur for protection. But now he was surrounded by the strange scent of tires. In the past few days, he had encountered countless new smells, and they made him nervous and irritable.

As he slept, he found himself curled up against the warm felt of the yurt's walls. He squirmed, tucking himself in closer. Later, still dreaming, he growled quietly. It was nighttime, and the snow was falling like a thick white curtain. He heard a strange sound. Mother Mastiff was leaving, and he howled into the night.

But Kelsang wasn't woken the next morning by the sound of a yak rising to its feet or the bleating of a sheep being milked. It was a bang that did it, as one of the guests let the metal gate swing back on its hinges as he left the guesthouse. This was no early morning out on the pastures.

Three days later a group of climbers gathered at Rong-buk Monastery, admiring the majesty of Mount Everest towering ahead and talking about a devilish black Tibetan mastiff, as they waited for the weather to improve.

4

LHASA'S STRAYS

FROM THE WINDOW of the jeep, Kelsang was mesmerized by the endless flow of people and cars on the street. Before long he spotted Master and sprang toward the door, ready to jump up on him. But to his great disappointment, it was another herdsman wearing a robe much like the one Tenzin usually wore. He began to notice other men wearing Tibetan robes, and even though not one of them was Master, seeing them made him feel that the grasslands were not too far away. A spark of hope reignited in his chest, even though most of the people on the street were dressed in thin, short jackets, like the men in the jeep.

If Kelsang hadn't been colorblind, he would have marveled at the variety of colors on display. This was Lhasa, and people traveled for thousands of miles to see its mysterious snow-clad landscape, as yet untouched by polluting hands, and its many manmade wonders — the Potala Palace, Jokhang Temple, Norbulingka. Some had made it their permanent home, but even more passed through temporarily on their way to the world's tallest mountain — Everest — where they sought fame by climbing to the top. People often perished at base camp from the effects of the altitude, yet still they went willingly, with smiles on their faces.

The streets of Lhasa were crawling with dogs. They were mostly mongrels who lounged in the afternoon sun at the doors of temples or under small stalls selling odds and ends. They were fed by pilgrims giving alms.

To Kelsang, this leisurely life of just waiting to be fed was unimaginable. He had woken up one morning with the impulse to herd a scattered flock of sheep on the grasslands, and ever since that day, he had somehow known that he was a shepherd dog. By day he helped Master herd the sheep out at pasture, and by night he kept guard back at the yurt, chasing away or killing any wolves who came near. It was as simple as that.

Kelsang was kept in a small courtyard for three days, and each day the two men brought him large chunks of mutton to eat. In those three days alone, he must have eaten the equivalent of an entire sheep. Most of the time, he lay in a corner and slept, and after a few days of rest and such hearty helpings of food, the discomfort and confusion that had accompanied him on the trip disappeared. The meat provided plenty of nourishment, giving him even stronger shoulder and chest muscles, much to the delight of his two feeders.

At dawn on the fourth day, Kelsang was led to the jeep,

a stick wedged beneath his collar. The jeep then carried him out of the dimly lit narrow alley and off to market.

He caused an instant disturbance as he was led into the wide open trading space built on the side of a mountain. He was led to his place among the other dogs, and very soon a crowd had gathered around him. There was no need for the tall skinny man or his companion to try to grab the customers' attention.

Kelsang noticed that the other dogs tied up here were much more like him than the weedy dogs on the street. There was a hodgepodge of all different kinds of mastiffs — golden yellow, white, bluey black, gray, even some rust red and an extremely rare coffee-colored one. And yet Kelsang was the only one over three feet tall and weighing more than 150 pounds — he was special even in a market full of mastiffs.

He tried to greet a bluey black mastiff sitting next to him, but it didn't even look up. Its coat had been carefully washed and brushed, giving it a finish as glossy as a bolt of raw silk. The mastiff traders were tired of dogs groomed until there wasn't a speck of dust on them. Indeed, these city mastiffs were nothing like the true mastiffs from the wilds — nothing like Kelsang. The bluey black mastiff's master pulled out a piece of meat in an attempt to animate his dog, but it ignored the treat and began to lick the fur on its leg like a cat lazing in the sun.

Everyone could see that Kelsang was different from these city-bred dogs. They pushed forward excitedly until they met his fearless gaze and then retreated. They could smell the wilds on this dog, whose fur stood on end, making him look even larger than he was. All the rest and rich food he had been getting meant that he was in excellent shape.

As the people gathered around, Kelsang had the feeling that something bad was about to happen. He crouched low on his thick post-like legs, shook his mane and growled.

The crowd edged farther back, beyond the reach of his shackles. The other dogs seemed tiny in comparison.

Suddenly a stick as thick as a wrist flew through the air toward Kelsang. Someone was testing him. Crraaaack! Two shards of wood flew back into the crowd. Kelsang had met the stick in midair and crunched through it in one bite. Gasps rose from the crowd as they dodged the remnants.

A beam of unnatural light, a snapping sound. Alarmed, Kelsang wanted to run away, but the tall skinny man and his friend pulled as hard as they could to detain him. A photographer had come to Lhasa to take pictures of local life. He shrank back, his face white with fright.

"That's no dog," he called out. "That's a lion!"

As a man with a long ponytail approached the tall skinny man to chat, Kelsang felt the chains around his neck suddenly go slack. They had been weighing on him ever since he left the grasslands. His master, Tenzin, had originally also fastened a chain around his middle for extra security, but it had worked loose in the jolting jeep, and the tall skinny man had obviously been too scared to refasten it.

His leather collar had fallen away. He had been wearing the collar for a year now, and all of his pulling and tugging over the past few days had taken their toll. The weakest part of it had snapped. Kelsang had grown used to having something weighing around his neck. In fact, he had come to see it as a natural part of his body. He felt uncomfortable without it, and in his confusion could only lean down to sniff the decaying collar now lying on the ground.

Someone called out in surprise, which shook Kelsang into action. He may have been from the depths of the northern grasslands, but he was used to having humans instruct him what to do. A shepherd dog doesn't need to think too much for himself. He just follows his master, tends the sheep out in the pasture, and as night falls, guards them in the camp. But now all decisions were up to him, and this one was important.

He stepped forward cautiously. Nothing happened. The chains didn't follow, nor did the clanking sound that had been his constant musical accompaniment. He took another step. No one said anything. No one knew what to do.

Kelsang made a decision — he had to get out of there — and he started jogging steadily toward the exit. Flustered, the tall skinny man called after him, but when Kelsang looked back, he fell silent. Everyone, including the other mastiffs, watched as he swaggered out of the market. Who would dare stop a mastiff straight from the grasslands?

Without thinking he set off for home.

But he was still in the middle of bustling Lhasa. Driven by instinct, he wound his way through the intricate pattern of alleyways until he could no longer see the large market and its imposing gate.

All over the city, small speckled mongrels were hanging around temples waiting for handouts. They never went hungry, and if they were bored, they simply scuttled into corners to make more little dogs. Their lives were so different from Kelsang's. He had purpose and only one goal, and that was to return to the grasslands.

He continued to make his way through the dark narrow alleys. Every now and then, frightened shouts greeted him, making him jump. People had reason to be scared. Kelsang didn't look like a dog. In fact, in no way did he seem like man's best friend. He was too big, too ferocious. Even though he slowed down whenever he encountered a pedestrian and ran past with his body close to the alley wall, his wild, aggressive look still terrified them. They would squeeze themselves up against the opposite wall, or else run away screaming as if they had seen a ghost.

This was terrifying for Kelsang, too. He approached a crowded street where people were selling dried meat and *tsampa* barley flour. The smells he had grown up with were everywhere, especially that of roasting flour. He unconsciously stopped in his tracks as he looked at

a stall stacked high with dried meat, but he was greeted with looks of shock and terror. The people here had
probably never seen a Tibetan mastiff wandering the
streets. They had no idea where he was from and pointed at him.

Kelsang turned into a small alley paved in stone. It
seemed to wind on forever, but he just kept running.

Someone started running behind him.

The man must have realized Kelsang's value — such
a fine Tibetan mastiff without a master! Even though he
himself might admit that trying to catch a mastiff was
a dangerous undertaking, when faced with the opportunity to make easy money — and a lot of it — there is
always someone stupid enough to try. The market for
other dogs had fallen in recent years, but not for Tibetan
mastiffs. These dogs were brave enough to take on wild
animals, and a purebred was worth thousands.

Being chased down a narrow alley would be enough to
scare any animal. Kelsang didn't know what was waiting
for him up ahead, but he knew that whoever was chasing
him was trying to make a grab for his tail. He ran as fast
as he could. He hadn't even put this much energy into
chasing that last wolf on the grasslands a few days before.

As he approached the end of the alley, Kelsang slipped
through an open door. It was the only way he could get
rid of his pursuer. He entered a small courtyard and
quickly found a dark recess to crawl into. He looked
around at the high walls, the many different flowers, the
lack of people.

His pursuer stopped dead at the courtyard door, then turned and stomped away. As far as he knew, the mastiff had found his way home.

Badly shaken, Kelsang did a lap of the courtyard and found a nice corner to lie down in. It was clean and quiet here. The cobbles had been worn to a shine by the passage of time, revealing beautiful veins like a rainbow in the stone. There was also a granite planter with flowers Kelsang had never seen before, and pots full of plants skirted the walls.

The quiet of the courtyard gave Kelsang a temporary feeling of safety, and he relaxed and dozed off. He got up only once during his long sleep to move out of the heat of the blazing sun and take refuge under a small tree, where he lay down and slept again. This was the first time he had felt safe enough to sleep properly since leaving the camp. The courtyard made him feel warm. He didn't want to leave, to go out again into streets full of strangers. Of course, he still longed for his camp on the grasslands, but he had no idea how he could get there without encountering all those curious people.

Kelsang awoke in the afternoon. But even while sleeping, he had been aware of everything going on around him. The door to the red building kept creaking, but that was only the tiniest of sounds that his sensitive ears had to strain to make out. It came at regular intervals, and because it had been there ever since Kelsang first entered the courtyard, he thought the door made this sound by itself. But when he awoke, he realized that this sound must belong to the courtyard's master. Kel-sang lay on the last bit of warm ground and waited for this new master to appear, trying to guess what he might look like based on his experiences of Lhasa so far.

He waited restlessly for what felt like ages. Eventually, he was distracted by the golden red of the Potala Palace and its brilliant gold roof. Out on the grasslands, he was always looking at nature's wonders, but this was the first time he had laid eyes on one made by man. He gazed at it in awe. The sun had left a smudge of red on the pal-ace's golden roof, making it look as if it were flushed from drinking. The cold, pale light of dusk made Kelsang think of the grasslands and the campsite crowded with sheep returning from pasture.

Just then he heard the heavy, deliberate steps he had been waiting for, and his muscles tightened. Don't move, he told himself, stay right where you are. After waiting for so long, Kelsang felt the urge to bite something. He clenched his jaws shut in an attempt to control the anxi-ety that was threatening to overwhelm him.

An old man with a reddish-brown Tibetan robe draped over his shoulders opened the door and shuffled into the courtyard. He was carrying a watering can cov-ered with flowers. He lifted his hand to shield his eyes from the sun's last rays, even though the light had start-ed to fade. Imagine how dark it must have been inside.

Kelsang had to fight his natural caution toward strangers, and breathing lightly, fixed on what he could only assume to be a weapon in the man's hands.

The man was very old, so old he had probably forgotten his own age. His face was crisscrossed with ravines, resembling layers of rock cracked and beaten by years of sun and wind. Only his eyes revealed any sign of life. He pulled a Tibetan blanket behind him as he watered the plants that had wilted in the fierce plateau sun. After he finished, he put the can down on the ground and sat on the reclining chair in the center of the courtyard, bringing him face to face with Kelsang.

Kelsang growled in that low, indignant way he had perfected. But he certainly wasn't interested in attacking this old man and would leave the moment he shooed him away. Kelsang's anger was born purely from despair. In a moment, he would have to face those strangers out on the street again.

But the old man looked at Kelsang as though he were merely a leaf that had blown into the courtyard. His gaze didn't linger longer than a moment. Then he lay back on his recliner.

The old man was silent and still. After glancing briefly at the dog, his shriveled eyes settled on the view of the Potala Palace over the top of the courtyard. He rested like this every day after painting his *tanka* scrolls, waiting for night to fall. Sometimes he would stay until the sky was full of stars.

Kelsang didn't know what to do. This man was different from the other people he had met that day. He didn't seem to care that there was a strange dog in his courtyard. In fact, he acted as if Kelsang had always been there, just like the flowers and plants. Perhaps Kelsang's nerves were playing tricks on him. Perhaps he had been living there for a long time. Dogs are easily affected by human emotions. Kelsang's muscles began to relax, but he didn't take his eyes off the painter. The old man didn't move. Indeed, he was as still as a stone wrapped in a blanket.

Everything in the courtyard was still.

Evening set in, and the old man's chair creaked as he sat up. Kelsang once again grew anxious, but the man just picked up his watering can and drifted back indoors. After a while, the door opened again, and he emerged carrying a bowl. He shuffled toward Kelsang and put it down in front of him before going back inside.

It was *tsampa* barley flour mixed with salty butter tea.

After Kelsang had finished, he looked up and saw a light shining from the second floor. As the courtyard door was open, he decided to take a walk. It was like being back on the grasslands. It was late, and there was no one about, so he stepped out of his alley into the next street. He walked even farther, crossing different alleys, and slowly approached Barkhor Street, which lay in the shadow of the Potala Palace.

Visible in the light of the summer moon were pilgrims who had come thousands of miles to prostrate themselves on the gray stones at this holy site. A sound like the patter of falling rain accompanied the methodical rise and fall of their bodies as their leather aprons slapped against the stones, which had been rubbed to a high gloss.

Kelsang was happy in the darkness. Temptation called to him, and he began to run, gliding like a spirit through dark recesses beyond the reach of moonlight. Even those most sensitive to their surroundings felt only the passing of a shadow as he ran by. A day of proper rest and a hearty bowl of food had restored his energy. All he wanted was to run through the narrow alleys and empty streets.

Kelsang suddenly slowed. The wind carried the smell of a pilgrim up ahead. As soon as the smell hit his nose, it awoke the memory of the distant grasslands in him once again. He stood in a corner inaccessible to the moon's rays and watched.

The pilgrim was moving along Barkhor Street with particular devotion, his hands pressed together in prayer, lifting his head and then laying himself flat upon the ground before standing up, taking a step and repeating the movements all over again. He was wrapped in a sheepskin robe that had become black and shiny with wear. His whole body gleamed in the moonlight like a rounded piece of stone.

To Kelsang, this man was the grasslands, and he could no longer control himself. He approached slowly and drew near before the man saw him. But the man's call was completely different from Master's, with a strange edge to it that cooled Kelsang's burning heart. He looked at the man's face covered in beads of sweat, and ignoring his calls, retreated into the dark.

Kelsang spent the entire night running around, blinded by his disappointment. People walking the streets only caught a glimpse of a gigantic black shadow flashing past before he disappeared around a corner.

"Must be seeing things," some of them mumbled to themselves.

Just as day was about to break, a hot, energetic Kelsang slipped into an alley behind the temple. He discovered it was a dead end and turned around. He should probably go back to the courtyard, he thought. The running had put him into a kind of trance, which tricked him into feeling soft grass beneath his paws.

A smudge of downy shadows had gathered at the entrance to the alley. The dawn light catching on their silhouettes made them sparkle like a glacier. The grass beneath Kelsang's feet instantly turned back to stone, bringing him out of his trance. He came to a stop, his breathing light, his rib cage rising and falling rhythmically.

A rabble of twenty dogs blocked his way up ahead, their eyes shining like wolves in the night. Kelsang was used to living on his own in the grasslands. He had never been around so many dogs of different shapes and colors, nor was he interested in them. The sky was growing light, he was losing his cover, and all he wanted to do was return to the painter's courtyard.

But just as Kelsang was about to charge through them onto the main street, the dogs began to bark, creating a terrifying cacophony. They may not have been strong, but their barking reverberated around the alley like a tidal wave.

Encouraged by their own din, they swarmed toward the hapless intruder. They were no longer the charming, gentle-looking dogs who lay around the temples in the daytime. They jostled together like a cluster of hairy spiders baring sharp teeth. There were so many of them, they had to run in two or three rows to fit into the narrow lane. Yet despite their crazed barking and dripping saliva, they didn't charge at him. It simply wasn't a suitable location to launch such an attack.

Kelsang was amazed — the tallest among them only came up to his chest. Could they really be making this earth-shattering sound? What surprised him even more was that the three strongest dogs at the front didn't understand even the basics of how to protect themselves. He could see at least five vulnerable spots, and yet they continued to thrust their faces forward, seemingly oblivious to the danger they were in. Kelsang was sure he could bite through the front leg of their leader, a blond lionesque dog.

A feeling of superiority washed over him as he watched the mindless barking mutts. He knew if any of them were to face a wolf out on the grasslands, they would be killed in a single chomp. These dogs were all bark and no bite, and they bored him.

Tilting his shoulder downward, he walked into the blond dog at the front as he prepared to leave the alley. The dog made no move to counterattack and screeched in pain.

But Kelsang was being careless, and a black-and-white dog, perhaps itself descended from a Tibetan mastiff, suddenly appeared at his side and tore into his shoulder. Kelsang's muscles tightened and turned as hard as stone, but he felt nothing beneath his long fur.

Even so, he roared with anger like a lion disturbed during his feed. The other dog realized what a formidable opponent he was before it had even spat out the mouthful of fur. Kelsang was clearly no ordinary neighborhood dog.

Kelsang easily knocked the black-and-white dog back into place. He barely had to make an effort as he sank his teeth into its neck, breaking it with just two sharp shakes. He tossed the floppy dog aside, the blood reminding him of his nights killing wolves. His desire to fight was like a wild fire spreading through his veins. Fear made the hair on the back of his neck stand on end, and from deep in his throat he let out a bloodthirsty roar.

The city dogs had never seen a massacre like this before. They usually only had to gang up on an intruding dog and knock it around a bit. They were scared senseless. A small bitch approached the dead dog and whimpered sorrowfully, while the others stood rooted to the spot, unsure what to do. One of them howled and turned away.

Then the dogs fled in every direction, like a river flooding over broken banks, leaving the blood-soaked corpse behind. Kelsang had once again demonstrated the undeniable superiority of his breed.

The sounds of early risers opening their front doors

began to fill the alleyway. Kelsang licked the drying blood from the corner of his mouth and left. When he got back to the courtyard, the door was still open, and all was quiet inside. He snuck in and lay down in his corner.

A young girl entered the courtyard that afternoon, when the sun was at its strongest. Kelsang had heard her turn into the alley and pricked up his ears, wondering if she was going to come in.

He had already begun to think of the courtyard as his own. It was still unfamiliar in some ways, but his instincts were telling him to protect it — the instincts that had been given to him by his ancestors. He had been away from the camp for so long that the courtyard had become its replacement. Kelsang imagined that he had always guarded this camp. He had no interest in the actual campsite or the sheep on it. He was driven by instinct — that was all — and this courtyard was the painter's camp.

Kelsang watched as a pair of leather shoes stepped across the threshold before jumping to his feet. He took up his position by the door and growled. He wasn't going to let the girl come in.

A scream as sharp as broken glass. The girl jumped back down the steps and ran out into the alleyway.

Even though he had successfully prevented her from coming in, Kelsang waited with some trepidation for the painter to appear. He barked, his eyes fixed on the door of the two-story red house. Had he done the right thing?

He wasn't sure, and he didn't know what to do next. If he had been on the grasslands, his master, Tenzin, would have come out of the yurt and tied him up to the wooden post.

The sound of a door opening. The old man stood in the doorway holding a paintbrush. It had taken great effort to tear his attention away from the colorful painting he had been working on. He seemed confused. Perhaps he was trying to remember if Kelsang was in fact his dog.

"Granddad, get rid of it!" The girl in the alley had also caught sight of the old man.

The painter's lips twitched. "It's okay."

Having expected this moment, the hair on the back of Kelsang's neck settled down, and he stalked back to his corner. Even though the old man's face was as expressionless as stone, Kelsang sensed that he had done the right thing. Feeling happy with himself, he lay down, but his fiery red eyes were still fixed on the young girl leaning through the courtyard door.

"Granddad, where did you find it?" The girl came in. She was carrying a small knapsack, and she cowered behind the old man, looking at Kelsang.

"He found me."

The painter's granddaughter, Drolma, came once a week to see him. Kelsang could detect the smells of food and pigments coming from her bag.

The next time she came to visit, Kelsang put up only a symbolic show of resistance, standing by the door and growling sluggishly, more as a way of letting the old man know that she had arrived than anything else. After leading Drolma into the courtyard, he went back to his corner.

Kelsang seemed to interest Drolma more than he did her grandfather. She tried feeding him a piece of dried meat directly from her hand, but it turned out to be a tiring process for both of them. Kelsang may have come to see her as part of the old man's property, but he still couldn't let down his guard completely. Drolma was equally cautious as she approached the huge dog, but she was determined nevertheless.

Not knowing what to do, Kelsang watched her edge toward him, crossing over the imaginary boundary he usually kept against strangers. The meat brushed up against his nose, but still he didn't move. Drolma was so nervous, her nose was dotted with beads of sweat. She bent down and placed the meat in Kelsang's metal bowl.

Then she went up to the second-floor balcony, which was so crammed with flowers it was like standing in a small flowerpot. She could see that the meat had disappeared, but Kelsang was lying in just the same position, as if he had never moved.

"Granddad, does the dog just lie there all day? Doesn't he ever go out?"

"I've never seen him move," the old painter answered, his eyes fixed on his latest *tanka*.

Of course Kelsang went out, but the old man just didn't know it. Every day when he went to water the flowers on his balcony, before he let his gaze wander up to the golden roof of the Potala Palace, he would look down on the dog below, lying motionless in the corner. Occasionally, the old man would muster a rare moment of energy and call out to Kelsang, rousing him from what appeared to be a deep sleep. Kelsang would jump up, run to the house and stare up at him, his amber eyes glinting in the sunlight. Not knowing what to do next, the old man would respond, "It's okay," and Kelsang would trot back to his corner, thudding back to the ground.

The next time the old painter went to feed Kelsang, he left him a *kha gdan*, a handmade Tibetan mat.

When night fell, and the roar of traffic and commotion on the street subsided, Kelsang would rouse from his deep sleep and look up, his eyes burning furiously in the dark. He would walk out of the courtyard door — the old man never closed the door — into the silent streets of Lhasa spread out beneath his feet.

Ever since he lost his job tending the sheep on the grasslands, Kelsang took to running aimlessly through the streets with an almost mad passion, trying to expend the energy he stored up during the day. His running began to take on a particular pattern, following a series of circles emanating from the painter's courtyard. After finishing one circuit, Kelsang would go back to the courtyard and look up at the silhouette of the painter in the second-floor window, where he often stood painting through the night, just to check that all was well before starting on a new circuit.

In the years that followed, Kelsang became a legend among the pilgrims of Lhasa, who honed their descriptions of the dark shadow they encountered and spread their stories far and wide. A pair of eyes watched them as they spun their prayer wheels and prostrated themselves on the cold paving stones around Jokhang Temple, but they weren't sure what it was, and it was gone by the time they looked up.

Kelsang would gaze with affection at the herdsmen draped in thick fur-lined robes who traveled here from the distant grasslands. But he always did so from deep in dark corners, and as soon as the men sensed he was there, he ran away.

He encountered many small dogs on his explorations of the city, but since none was a match for him, he almost never slowed down, preferring instead to breeze by. He once bit two dogs who tried to pick fights with him, and after that, the other dogs fled as soon as they saw him coming. But this was Lhasa, a place where anything could happen. No one could guarantee that there wasn't an even more exceptional mastiff in another courtyard somewhere. Kelsang was not invincible.

One coal-black night, Kelsang came across his first real opponent since leaving the grasslands. He left the courtyard, as usual, and started to trot around the city. As his body began to warm up, he spotted a silvery gray wolfhound flickering in the evening light up ahead. He slowed down. Was it a German shepherd, a mastiff or a St. Bernard?

The wolfhound had no intention of running away and stared as Kelsang approached, its eyes fluorescent with purpose, like a wolf stalking a sheep. This dog was different from the yappy ones Kelsang had encountered recently. Growling softly, the wolfhound raised its head and started to walk forward in a determined fashion, its tail as erect as a tree trunk. Its lips were pulled back to reveal a set of sharp white teeth, its wolverine ears were pressed close to its head, and its red eyes were fixed fearlessly on Kelsang. It looked even bigger than the mastiff.

Having fought with more than one wolf on the grasslands, and with other dogs since, Kelsang was not inclined to think well of the wolfhound. And yet he had no desire to start a fight. He turned slightly and slipped past, growling a warning to the other dog not to get too close. His muscles were tight and ready to spring into action.

But before the wolfhound had time to react, a reflex made Kelsang twist right around and sink his teeth into its neck. They clashed in midair, their teeth grinding, their paws grabbing at each other's torsos. As soon as he landed back on the ground, Kelsang pulled away. This was the first time he had encountered such a worthy opponent since arriving in the city — he had nearly been knocked to the ground. After a brief pause, they clashed again. Since they were roughly the same build, Kelsang decided not to make a tactical withdrawal, but instead charged forward with all his might. The other dog was of the same mind and met Kelsang like a lump of rock.

They crashed into each other again and again, biting and scratching. Kelsang was about to bite into the wolf-hound's right leg, but his opponent was quick and was already poised to bite his shoulder. Instead it twisted farther and went for his neck, forcing Kelsang to refrain from biting and shrug it off.

They pulled apart and stood eyeing each other. The wolfhound was also clearly surprised to have encountered such a valiant challenger.

A loud cracking sound. Everything, even the air, was shaking, and for a few moments Kelsang couldn't hear anything. The flagstones around him split, sending flying splinters up his nose. This wasn't the first time he had been deafened by such a sound. Back at the guesthouse, out on the grasslands, when he had been forced to fight those two dogs, a sound just like this one had rung out, killing one of them. He had been shocked by the vibration but hadn't fully understood its power.

Now he understood. He barked in anger. Where had the sound come from? Before he could determine the answer, there was another explosion right beside his head, and another slab of stone cracked open. Such an almighty force. The wolfhound clearly knew what was happening as it darted toward the shadows. Kelsang did the same, running out of the alley in the opposite direction.

Another gun shot.

When they realize that their time is up and the fear of death takes hold, most dogs will let out a howl that summons all their inner strength. It's their only way to express their love of life. For the rest of his days Kelsang would tremble whenever he recalled this terrible sound.

He stood in the shadows, the long hair on the back of his neck standing on end. The wolfhound had been hit squarely in the back but was still scrapping with its absent opponent under the streetlight. The gnashing of its teeth echoed around the alleyway like the sound of iron being filed. It looked like a giant squirming insect as it struggled to drag itself to the other side of the street using only its forelegs, its hind legs already paralyzed. Windows lit up along the alley as the howling woke its inhabitants.

Kelsang believed that howl must have risen from the depths of hell itself. He was too scared to move from his corner. Another shot came whistling past.

He couldn't control the shaking that came from deep within him. Fear was eating away at his strength. He had to escape. If he waited any longer, he would be drowned by this sound, and that thought was more chilling than the coldest winter on the plateau. It was enough to make his heart burst.

He started running, hiding in places where the light didn't reach. If there had been anyone in his path, he would have bumped them out of the way. He had already rounded two corners, yet the sound was everywhere, ringing in his ears, driving him insane. He could only keep running.

The howling wolfhound let out a cough that sounded

like cloth tearing and then fell silent, as if it had suddenly fallen into deep water.

Kelsang careered into the courtyard and plopped down on his mat. It smelled like he did, and it comforted him. He stared at the half-open door, panting heavily. The haunting sound hadn't followed him, but still, once his breathing became calm, he decided to make sure. There was silence in the alley outside. It was empty. The light in the painter's window was still on.

Kelsang thought back to the events at the guesthouse and then thought about the last half hour. Guns were terrifying weapons, he concluded, with their smoke and devastatingly loud sounds. And they belonged to humans. A gun had taken away that dog's life, but he had been lucky — the other bullet hadn't got him.

The next day, in a shop that sold sweetened Tibetan tea, a loquacious man bragged to his friends that he had almost shot a small black lion the night before. The lion had been fighting a stray. No one believed him, of course. The last time, he claimed he'd shot an elephant through the ear, all because the elephant had found nighttime in the holy city too boring and had gone for a walk.

Kelsang stayed in the courtyard for the next few evenings, the events in the alley still lingering in his thoughts. But on the third night, feeling confined and depressed, he decided to venture out again. He was a shepherd dog, and while Lhasa had no sheep for him to tend, he still had to do something to relieve the urge to run.

He was more cautious than before, however. He stayed close to the alley walls, refusing to stray into the moonlight where he would be accompanied by his own shadow. He kept his nose up in the air as he ran, sniffing out new smells from the daytime activity in the city.

Perhaps it was just a coincidence, but Kelsang found himself back in the same alley as the other night. He edged down its walls, faltering, sniffing at the air and listening for hidden dangers. Finally, he reached the street-light.

The dog's corpse had been cleaned away, yet Kelsang could detect a trace of blood among numerous other smells. He found the red-smeared bullet lodged in a corner, locking the smell of blood and smashed lead deep in his memory. He didn't know why he had come. He flared his agitated nostrils, breathing in the dog's blood as well as a myriad other smells, including human urine and the sweet fragrance of shampoo, which came from one of the sheep that had been cleaned and left to roam the city as a spiritual offering to Buddha.

Kelsang stayed in the shadows for a couple of minutes, careful to stay well hidden. Then he began to run again, deciding to leave everything to do with that dog far behind. He would continue to run these streets, but from now on he would be more secretive, more careful. These experiences were maturing. In fact, they were proof that he had already adjusted to life in the city.

As day broke, he was drawn to a familiar scent, or

rather he was seduced by it. Unable to control himself, he ran toward its source, squinting his eyes. Two sheep were grazing on a small patch of grass up ahead. His nose had been seized by their smell, even though it was not entirely the one he was used to. They had been cleaned so vigorously that not a trace of dirt could be found in their wool, and they shone like fine white silk. They were covered in red and green silk ribbons and were absorbed in munching the grass.

When Kelsang approached, their reaction was all too familiar. Showing no sign of fear, but rather overwhelming acceptance, they huddled together looking at him meekly.

Only when he was right in front of the sheep did Kelsang realize that he didn't know what to do or where to herd them. There was no shepherd, no campsite and no flock. This was the city, with concrete and stone as far as the eye could see.

A strange chemical smell wafted from their wool. These were not the sheep of the grasslands that he knew so well. He felt strange seeing these sheep here in Lhasa, so far away from the camp — so strange that he had to run away. There were just two of them — this was not the flock that he had been longing for.

Kelsang was to see many more such sheep, but after that first encounter, he kept his distance. He lost the urge to rush toward them and round them up. They, too, were aimless, solitary creatures since leaving the grasslands.

Kelsang now knew his way around Lhasa — at night,

at least. He began to leave his scent on easily distinguish-
able landmarks, such as a streetlight or a stone by the
entrance to an alley. He would go back the next day and
sniff each one carefully. Only rarely did he discover the
scent of another dog. Usually dogs trying to assert themselves recoiled at his strong, wild smell. Sometimes, in a
moment of mischief, a stray would make a half-hearted
attempt to leave its scent on top of Kelsang's and then
never dare to appear in that part of the city again. Almost all of Lhasa's strays avoided him. He only brought
disaster.

Kelsang had his own forbidden areas of the city. At
least, he never returned to the alley where the wolfhound was shot. Even though he had grown accustomed
to hiding in the shadows when he ran, he knew that guns
hid even in dark corners. He would never return to that
place — danger lurked there.

Kelsang had settled into city life. But although he was
a Tibetan mastiff, he was still, after all, a dog. He needed a place to stay and a master. The old painter was the
perfect person to fill such a role. If the weather was particularly good, the old man would take a break from his
painting and go out into the courtyard wearing a pair of
sunglasses. He would then settle into his chair. Kelsang
didn't feel close to him. The painter hadn't said much
since Kelsang first appeared in the courtyard, nor had he
even looked at him properly. But the old man did come
every day at the same time with a bowl of milky butter
tea mixed with *tsampa* barley flour. In the painter's eyes,

there was no difference between feeding Kelsang and watering his flowers. Kelsang was a small seed that had been blown in by the wind and had quietly taken root.

Kelsang didn't expect intimacy. As long as he had a master, in some sense of the word, then he was happy. And when it came to life in the city, the old painter was as perfect a master as he could wish for.

Not many people in Lhasa knew that such a talented painter lived in the Tibetan-style two-story house. The old man had no friends, and apart from the person who came once a month to deliver his pigments, his only visitor was his granddaughter, Drolma. No one knew how old he was. The painter hardly came into contact with the outside world.

The small house was also home to two priceless thirteenth-century *tanka* paintings. The master's own paintings were art treasures, too, and some of them had even been commissioned for temples within the Potala Palace itself. Visitors who came from afar to the incense-filled temples marveled at their beautiful colors and ingenious compositions. Young art students came year after year to gaze at the *tankas*, astonished by their quality. "I'd stay here and live on stale bread and water for weeks just to keep looking at them," they'd exclaim. Not even the altitude dissuaded them from lingering for hours before the old man's masterpieces. Only when night fell and the temples were closing would they pick up their backpacks and head to a youth hostel for the night. They had no idea that their creator was still living and working on even more paintings in a small red house down a quiet alley nearby.

The old painter himself probably didn't know the real value of his paintings. He simply sat before his easel and painted the old stories before they were lost forever. Which two colors would go best together? That was all he cared about.

But there was someone else who knew.

It was a still night with no moon.

Other dogs never wandered into the alley because it was where Kelsang lived. They knew that the giant dog only slunk around in the shadows of darkness and that it was safe during the day. But even so, they avoided it because of Kelsang's presence — the smell of the wilderness that he left there.

The neighbors had no idea that such a dog lived with the painter, and his habit of going out only at night meant that his presence remained a secret, buried in the depths of the alley.

Kelsang had nearly finished his circuit and was approaching the entrance to his alley. Usually a soft light would be shining from the second-floor window, and he could then set off for another round about the city. But as he drew closer, he smelled something strange permeating the sun-dried stones. It was a mixture of cigarette smoke, alcohol and sweet tea, and it made him feel uncomfortable.

Kelsang shook his head. He had been so content just moments ago, and now he was desperate to get rid of this unpleasant smell. But he couldn't have his way. He was a dog with an acute sense of smell living in one of the cleanest parts of the city. The smell wasn't going to go away just because he wanted it to.

Suddenly he heard strange noises in the dark, as if they were confirming the presence of the new smell. Even though to Kelsang, the alley belonged to his master, life in the city had taught him a few things. He didn't rush forward straight away but hid in the dark, waiting to discover the source of the noise.

"Are you sure nothing's going to go wrong?"

It was only a whisper from a dark corner of the alley, but Kelsang still heard it.

"Nothing's going to go wrong. The old man lives alone. I've been watching the place and there's no one else. The girl only comes once a week."

"Really?"

"Really."

"I'm still a bit scared."

"There's nothing I can do about that. It's just the old man, and he's so old, he's fossilizing. All we have to do is flash our knives, and the old codger will hand over the paintings. Remember what the guy said? It doesn't matter how big they are. As long as we get them to him, he'll give us ten thousand *yuan*."

"Ten thousand *yuan*, ten thousand *yuan*…" The cowardly voice was trying to take in what it would mean. The other one swore quietly as he stumbled over a stone. The tiny sound was like a clap of thunder. The two men nervously dropped to the ground and were still. They didn't see Kelsang slip past them into the courtyard as if he were one with the night.

The courtyard belonged to Kelsang, and he wouldn't allow it to be violated. Yet he wasn't going to provoke the two men out in the alley. Experience told him he shouldn't attack first. But what made him feel extra uncomfortable was the faintest whiff of iron in the air. Were they carrying a gun?

As soon as the men entered the courtyard, not even Kelsang's fear of guns could suppress his guarding instinct. The first man was so focused on the house, now completely dark, that when he heard the warning close to his ear, his mind went blank. But he knew it was the growl of an angry, vicious beast. He swiveled, unconsciously raising an iron bar to his head.

As Kelsang's teeth met the iron bar, the sound of grinding metal filled the courtyard. Another attack followed straight afterward. Kelsang couldn't smell gunpowder, so he knew he was safe. The iron bar might be capable of damage, but it wasn't a gun. His fears melted away, and he launched himself at the man in what turned out to be a completely one-sided fight.

A wail of pain cut through the night like a blunt knife. Window after window lit up as the crying grew even louder. A few people appeared in the alley, but they were too scared to go and see what was happening inside the painter's courtyard. They knew from the terrified screams that it was something truly horrific.

The old painter got up slowly, switched on the light and put on his red robe. By the time he got outside, it was already dawn and the noises had petered out. But as long as the people in the alley held their breath, they could still make out a low groaning. They had been peeping through a crack in the door, and when they saw the old painter, they pushed it open and poured into the courtyard.

The neighbors had glimpsed a Tibetan mastiff crouching in the dark and could now see it more clearly. They gasped at its humungous size. But Kelsang wasn't paying any attention. He was staring intently at two slabs of stone that had been there for goodness knows how long. Faint cries of help were coming from behind them.

An iron bar, a Tibetan knife covered in blood and scraps of clothing lay on the ground.

Kelsang kept his gaze fixed on the crack between the stones while occasionally licking his shoulder. He had been injured. When he leapt toward the man with the iron bar, the other man came from behind with a knife in hand. Sensing a shadow coming at him, Kelsang twisted his body in midair and bit the man's sleeve. He felt a sharp sting on his shoulder. With all the strength he could muster, he ripped the clothes straight off the man's back. He cast the scraps of clothing on the ground and bit into the wrist holding the knife. The tip of the knife nicked the skin on his shoulder.

The old painter was confused to see so many people in his courtyard. Perhaps the characters from his latest *tanka* had come to life. The neighbors were also surprised. For many years, they'd thought this courtyard was empty. Only those older than the painter himself seemed to remember him. They were not only surprised to see the old man but were equally shocked by the mastiff. No one could remember ever hearing a dog barking in the alley. It was unbelievable. But then again, was it? This was Lhasa, after all.

Even up until the moment the police arrived, the painter didn't understand exactly what had gone on. But he still called Kelsang, and with some reluctance, the dog stood up, made his way to the corner and lay down on his mat. But his eyes didn't move from the crack between the two slabs of stone.

There were two people hiding behind the stones, even though the opening looked barely wide enough for a cat to fit through. No one could figure out how they got in there. But the two men were rejoicing in their good luck. Heaven, in all its grace, had given them shelter to hide from the demon dog. If their only escape had been a mouse hole, they would have squeezed themselves into it. They had scraped their bottoms as they wiggled between the slabs, but once curled up inside they were like hibernating marmots. They blocked up part of the crack with stones, and neither could think of a more wonderful place on earth.

No matter how much the policemen threatened and

cajoled, the two men refused to come out of their fortress. Perhaps they thought they were being tricked, and that as soon as they came out people would set that thing on them again. Yes, "That thing!" was exactly how they referred to Kelsang.

They still didn't know what had attacked them. The two policemen told them it was a Tibetan mastiff, but they didn't believe them.

"Aren't mastiffs dogs? No way. Whatever attacked us wasn't a dog."

They were prepared to confess that they had been trying to steal the *tankas*, which pleased the policemen. An open and shut case. But it still took half an hour to convince the men to come out. The policemen were growing impatient, as was everyone else in the courtyard, and they eventually threatened to set fire to the hiding place. The men agreed on one condition — only as long as "That thing" was either tied up or put in a cage. Only then would they come out.

No one wanted to go near Kelsang, who had been growling the whole time in accompaniment to the rising and falling of the crowd's voices. Furthermore, the rising and falling of the hair on the back of his neck suggested he might attack again at any moment. The painter fetched some rope and tied one end around Kelsang's neck and the other end to a tree. He didn't give the situation much thought. All he wanted was to get back to his usual peace and quiet. It was already time for him to be painting.

As the painter tied the rope around his neck, Kelsang hesitated. Should he really be submitting like this? But he was a dog, and dogs don't go against the will of their master, no matter how temporary that master is. So he yielded as the painter tightened the rope.

What happened next convinced the impatient on-lookers that the time spent waiting had been worth it.

First, a hand popped out.

Kelsang leapt to his feet, but the rope pulled as taut as the string of a musical instrument, and the force shook the tree so hard that a dusting of green leaves fell to the ground. He howled furiously and continued pulling.

The hand whipped back into the hole like a fright-ened snake.

After more negotiation, the two men eventually emerged. Out came two feet wearing heavy boots. What came next made the crowd guffaw, and even the usu-ally expressionless painter laughed. A shiny white bot-tom covered with red cuts and scratches wormed its way backwards out of the crack. Aside from his boots, the man was completely naked.

"Look, it's like he's just come out of his mother's tum-my!" There was a roar of laughter, even louder than the first.

The other man came out, and his appearance was no more dignified. But the two men weren't bothered by the laughter coming from the spectators. In fact, they looked full of joy as the policemen handcuffed them. Somehow they had managed to survive.

The old painter was attentive to Kelsang's food over the next few days, but somehow he forgot to untie the rope around his neck. Perhaps he had forgotten that Kelsang was not a plant. The truth was that nothing in the world mattered to the old man except his *tankas*, and they took every bit of his energy.

As darkness fell on the second evening of being tied up, Kelsang stood up quietly. The night was calling to him, but the rope wouldn't let him go. He tried pulling at it. It was made of hemp and shouldn't be too strong. But the painter had used a slipknot, so that every time Kelsang pulled, the noose became tighter. The small tree to which the other end was tied was extremely tough and flexible, capable of bearing the strain. He pulled several times, but each time the rope grew so tight he could scarcely breathe. He had no option but to give up.

By the morning of the third day, Kelsang was about to explode with pent-up frustration. He was a shepherd dog, and he needed exercise. The worst of it was that he could hear the yapping of other dogs in the alleys nearby. Perhaps his scent around the city had begun to fade.

But it was the visitors who really changed life for Kelsang and the painter. The story spread quickly of the enormous Tibetan mastiff who had driven two knife-wielding thieves into a hole barely large enough for a cat in order to protect his master and his priceless paintings. People wanted to see this dog for themselves. They gathered in the alley and even climbed onto the wall, sending loose bricks to the ground as they tried to catch a glimpse of him.

Kelsang had no way to vent his anger at such improper behavior but to howl. These days everything made him bark — the faces looking at him over the wall, the eyes peeking through the cracks in the door, the strange footsteps in the alley. Spit drooled from the corner of his mouth as he jumped over and over again, only to be pulled back by the tree. It was as if he had gone crazy.

But everything he did only elicited more cries of admiration — such a beautiful, magnificent dog!

The day after the attempted robbery, the old painter did something he had never done before. He locked the courtyard door. But then the strangers began to knock. They waited patiently, admiring the antique bronze knockers shaped like animal heads before clanking them loudly again and again, until the painter had no choice but to answer. After marveling at the dog, who clearly only wanted to pounce on them, they all, without exception, asked if he was for sale. Maybe the old painter didn't understand, or maybe he had other reasons, but he always just asked them to leave in his characteristically terse manner. He was always stony faced, and it was clearly pointless to try to discuss anything with a statue. But eventually, the painter became just as irritated as Kelsang with all the interruptions.

"Don't be angry with me, little dog," he said to Kelsang one day. This was the most he had ever said to him.

Kelsang could see from the old man's face that his

fate was about to change. From the moment the chubby, dark-cheeked man entered the courtyard — it was as if every ray of the plateau sun had graced those cheeks — the change in the old painter's countenance was obvious. His stony face seemed to flex slightly, and he turned suddenly to look at Kelsang. It was only a glance, but Kelsang stood up involuntarily in an attempt to understand exactly what was going on. He had been here for quite some time, but despite being right under the old man's nose, he had never been treated as anything more important than a plant.

"If you like him, take him," the old man said to the dark-cheeked visitor staring at Kelsang.

The man didn't understand what the old painter meant. Someone at lunch that day had told a story about an exceptional mastiff and the hilarious way he had captured two thieves, which sent the whole restaurant into fits of laughter. None of the diners thought to check if the owner had actually been there to witness what happened. The story was too good to ruin with such nitpicking. But the dark-cheeked man made straight for the alley. As soon as he saw Kelsang lying in the corner, he knew what a rare, beautiful mastiff he was. He trembled with excitement, and all he could think of was how to get the wizened old man to let him in for a closer look.

"What?" He couldn't believe his ears. He watched the huge dog stretch out slowly.

"He's yours. Take him." Words were an extravagance to the old painter, who was so used to being alone. They were only to be spoken when absolutely necessary. But he repeated himself, and this time the man understood.

The mastiff belonged to him!

Lhasa was that kind of place. You had no idea what was going to happen under that bright blue sky. The coin you bought might turn out to be priceless. Perhaps the girl walking toward you, whose beauty made you forget everything else, was descended from the Nepalese nobility. Lhasa, the city of the sun, where you had no idea what tomorrow would bring, where people came from miles around to chase their dreams.

The man felt the blood rise in his chest. I've been here for years now, he said to himself. This isn't altitude sickness. I must just be a bit excited.

Since the man wasn't moving, the painter went over to the tree, untied the rope and put it in his hand. Then he turned and shuffled into the house without looking back. His *tanka* needed just a few more daubs of paint, and then it would be finished.

Kelsang had to make a difficult decision. Having spent the last few days tied up and only able to move a few feet, he had already begun to feel his muscles wasting away, and he had been overcome with fear. How long could he go on like that? The most important thing at this point was to leave the small courtyard from which he could only see the blue sky and the golden top of the Potala Palace. If that hadn't been the case, Kelsang would never have let himself be led away by a stranger with a rope around his neck.

The painter didn't even look at him, but Kelsang had experienced that before, and it certainly didn't make him feel sad or aggrieved. The painter was no more important than a plant to Kelsang. Guarding his courtyard and fending off the thieves had only been a matter of instinct. If Kelsang were to protest, he would probably be allowed to stay, but then nothing much would change for him.

Kelsang could feel the man's fear through the rope, and he could smell it, too. He wanted to get out of the courtyard, and so he let himself be led away. But his own obedience shocked him slightly. He followed the man with his smell of gasoline, smoke and food out into the alley.

Lhasa at dusk. But Kelsang didn't have time to look around. He was too busy enjoying the feeling of his swollen paws against the cold stone slabs. His sudden appearance attracted many surprised looks. Apart from that first day, he had only ever wandered at night when the day's smells had already begun to dissipate. He sniffed greedily and stored these new smells deep in his memory.

They approached a truck with a khaki green canvas cover in the parking lot behind the market. The smells of the day's trading were drifting away, leaving only the slightest lingering trace.

The man pulled out a forked stick and slid it under the rope around his neck, but Kelsang was so caught up in all the new smells that he didn't react. He could still detect the man's fear, and frightened humans weren't dangerous as far as he was concerned.

But as soon as the stick was lodged firmly in place, the fear that had been emanating from the man began to disappear, jolting Kelsang to his senses. He knew from the man's laughter that it was too late. The stick was over two yards long, and it kept a secure distance between them. No matter how much he barked and bit, Kelsang had no way of getting close to the man. It didn't take him long to realize that such efforts would be futile. He remained calm, wanting to know what was going to happen next. Previous experience had taught him that there was no point in wasting energy on useless struggle.

Kelsang was led into the truck, and the other end of the stick was tied firmly to a bar inside, restricting him to a gloomy corner at the back. He could lie down, but his neck had to remain upright, resting against the icy cold side of the vehicle. Cardboard boxes and other odds and ends were scattered around in the back, giving off unpleasant smells. Kelsang began to sneeze again and again, and with each sneeze, the rope around his neck grew a bit tighter.

He regretted not escaping earlier. He could have easily bitten through the rope that had tied him to the tree, but he had been observing some kind of pact between the canine and human worlds. Maybe he should have bitten through the rope as he was being led into the alley, but it was too late now. He had no way of removing the stick wedged under the rope at his neck, no matter how hard he tried.

The truck drove all night until they reached a small town just before dawn.

Kelsang was led out of the truck and up a mountain slope on a trail that went behind a large building. Four or five people surrounded him as they climbed in the first light of day. He knew what was about to happen — he could feel the impatience in the air. He tried with all his might to pounce on the man with the dark cheeks, but he only managed to push him back as the man grappled with the other end of the stick.

A series of lassos came whistling toward Kelsang. He jumped to dodge them, but the man on the other end of the stick prevented him from getting away. One after the other, the lassos landed around his neck before they were quickly pulled tight. Bewildered, Kelsang thrashed about, stepping on one of the ropes around his neck and pulling it even tighter. Soon he lay panting on the ground like a rice dumpling wrapped in a leaf and criss-crossed with string.

These men had done this before. Within minutes they slipped a steel-reinforced leather collar around his neck, screwed a five-yard-long metal chain to it and cut off the ropes.

Kelsang stood up only to find that he was now attached by a set of chains to a pole screwed into the ground. Once everything was in order, the last man edged back slowly. He suddenly dislodged the stick wedged under Kelsang's collar and ran away. Kelsang was not about to give up this opportunity and let out a whole night's worth of pent-up anger as he began to howl, scratching at the man's shadow.

The man was so frightened he fell to the ground but quickly scrambled to his feet again to a chorus of shouting. His face was ash white, and his leather jacket lay in tatters at his feet. It hadn't taken long for Kelsang to overtake his two-yard head start.

"He's not bad, Boss. Much stronger than the last one."

"You don't come across one as good as this every year," the man with the dark cheeks replied. "I just didn't think I'd find him in the city. You usually only see the good ones in out-of-the-way places." He fished out a pile of bills from his wallet and handed them to the shivering man. "Buy yourself another jacket."

If only he'd escaped when he had the chance, Kelsang thought sorrowfully. He'd never get out of here now.

After the men left, Kelsang slowly calmed himself down. At least he was back on his long-lost beloved grasslands. And his sense of smell was returning after the torment of the journey. He could smell his collar, the metal chains, the wooden pole, the grass beneath his paws, and another mastiff.

Another mastiff. Kelsang spent the rest of the day thinking about this.

Even though he had a collar around his neck and was yet again weighed down by heavy chains, the most important thing was that he was back on the grasslands. All his memories of running around as a puppy suddenly came back to him. Dragging his heavy chains, he ran in circles around the pole barking madly, the grasslands spinning around him. Since his chains were fastened to the pole by a metal ring, he could run around like this as much as he liked.

From a distance, Kelsang looked like a seething ball of black fire galloping around on the slope. He didn't try to bite at his chains or the pole. That was obviously pointless.

The man with the dark cheeks stood outside the Sichuan restaurant at the edge of town watching his booty.

"*Om mani padme hum,*" he sighed, finding comfort in the Buddhist mantra.

Not long ago, that very pole had been home to another mastiff — a little one from a nearby farm. There was no comparing him to Kelsang, yet a man from Chengdu had bought him for thirty thousand *yuan*.

As dusk approached, the golden crown of the Potala Palace was once again bathed in the plateau's evening sun. The painter shuffled out into the courtyard carrying a bowl of milk mixed with *tsampa* barley flour. But Kelsang wasn't lying in the corner on his mat. The old man paused, pondered for a moment and then stooped to pick up the mat, which was covered in dog hair. All this thinking made him tired in a way he had never felt before, but eventually he came to a satisfactory conclusion. There had, in fact, never been a Tibetan mastiff in his courtyard. Deciding to give the matter no more thought, he walked to the door and emptied the contents of the metal bowl into the street. Stray dogs would come along later and lap it up. Then he threw the mat up against the wall and went back inside to paint.

That night the wind came and carried Kelsang's mat away. The next morning, the painter shambled out to water his plants. Kelsang had never existed, he was sure of it. While there was still a hazy image of a dog lingering in the back of his mind, he thought of it as he did one of his *tanka* paintings that had been taken away and was now hanging in a temple somewhere.

A few days later, someone arrived wanting to buy the famous mastiff, knocking and waiting patiently outside the door. But the old man — older than the carved stones that lined Bakor Street — said that there had never been such a dog.

It was as if none of it had ever happened.

5

MEETING HAN MA
IN THE WILDS

EVERY DAY A WAITER emerged from the big building at the foot of the mountain and threw a leg of mutton or half a rack of ribs to Kelsang, who was tied higher up on the mountainside. The man would then place a rusty bowl of water, filled to the brim, just within his reach.

No one dared approach Kelsang, not only because the boss had instructed them not to, but because he was becoming more and more wild. His resentful eyes had a cold, crimson stare. Everyone who saw him was convinced he would attack and bite off a leg, given the chance.

After he had eaten, he ran around the pole, plowing the grass within a five-yard radius as he attempted to release the energy he had stored up during the day. White shards of sheep bone were scattered all over the ground like the floor of a slaughterhouse that hadn't been cleaned in years.

Kelsang's coat no longer had its beautiful gloss, partly because of the constant rain and sleet of early autumn, but his body was also preparing for winter. His fur stuck out rudely at every angle, as if he'd been draped in a felt rug. From a distance, he looked twice his usual size, and anyone seeing him for the first time was convinced he was a bear.

Kelsang's only relief was to run around his pole. The earth around it was stamped with paw marks. Sometimes he would sit in front of the pole and look out at the bleak narrow town and the people walking around it. He barked at every car that stopped at the Sichuan restaurant down below. He didn't know why, but any new stimulus made his body tremble with excitement. Sometimes he even closed his eyes and leapt forward, tugging at his chains. The desire to chew and swallow everything he saw burned in his young chest.

Truck drivers would stop to fill up on spicy Sichuan food after their long, difficult day on the road. Once they'd scraped their plates clean, they would climb up the hill, belching bitter chili burps, to get a closer look at the monster who had barked at them as they drove into the parking lot. This quickly became part of the experience of eating at the bustling restaurant.

No one came close, but they all stood admiring Kelsang from afar, gazing in fascination at his blood-smeared mouth. Many of the truck drivers wanted to buy Kelsang, but the man with the dark cheeks was asking too high a price, and deal after deal failed. The men would drive off in different directions, but Kelsang's new owner wasn't worried. He knew there would be more people with whom he could bargain. He was in no rush. He simply couldn't let this fine mastiff go for anything less than the sum he was asking.

Even on the windiest, snowiest nights out on the Tibetan plateau, Kelsang could always find shelter behind the yurt in among the fleeces, but here he had nothing. Still, he was remarkably resilient in the violent snowstorms. The damp and cold only made him stronger and more determined. Early one morning, the people in the building woke to find three feet of snow blocking the door. They had no choice but to send one of the young waiters through a window to dig them out. To his amazement, the dog on the hill was running around in the dazzling white like a ball of fire, stirring up a cloud of snow around him.

Mastiffs are not naturally inclined to enjoy human company, yet Kelsang still found life on the slope lonely. His resentment drove him to bite anything he could, but there was nothing to satisfy his desire to attack. Any remaining sheep bones had long since been crunched to powder.

The man who fed Kelsang was becoming more frightened of him every day. Before the legs of mutton he threw even hit the ground, Kelsang jumped up and chomped them in two. His gnawing sounded like a hurricane as he quickly reduced the legs to tiny pieces, not so much from hunger as from his desire to feel his teeth tearing through flesh. When the man caught sight of Kelsang's bone-speckled muzzle and his sleepless amber eyes flickering in the jungle of his fur, he took a few steps back. Who knew what the dog was thinking.

Kelsang had lost hope of ever leaving this place, and besides, he was beginning to get used to it. He had been confined for so long that he had come to believe that the iron chains and leather collar, which had rubbed away revealing the metal cable underneath, were a natural part of his body.

Every night, when the moonlight shone down into the valley and all was quiet, Kelsang, no longer able to control the desire that had been welling up in him, would point his nose at the yellow sphere in the sky and howl with all his strength. Once he started, he would continue in broken gasps all through the night.

And so it was that Kelsang fell into the world of mastiff trading. From the moment he was taken from his home, he entered a world that he hadn't chosen and didn't understand. If the jeep hadn't driven up to the camp, he probably never would have left the grasslands. He would have grown old with the sheep, in green pastures under blue skies, just like other mastiffs. There would have been occasional fights with wild animals, and he would have killed some of them. And there would have been the chance — a very small chance — that he would have made a mistake and succumbed to an attack himself. But if he had lived long enough out on the grasslands, he would have been sure to continue his own pure mastiff bloodline.

But everything had changed. He had left that life forever, and never again would he be a shepherd dog. He had even lost the freedom to run the streets of Lhasa by night. As long as no other mastiff appeared, he was probably destined to remain tied up on this mountainside, to age slowly as the man with the dark cheeks dreamed of making it rich. Either that, or he would be bought by a wealthy man and spend the rest of his days guarding a mansion.

The rusty red mastiff was suffering the same treatment that Kelsang had. It was being led out of a truck by a long stick. It was already showing signs of age — the color of its coat was starting to fade and two clumps of bronzy-gold fur were sprouting above its eyes. As the helpers led the new mastiff down from the back of the truck, Kelsang noticed that their sleeves were slathered in blood.

But this mastiff was eerily calm. It didn't react as the loops of rope hurtled over its head, not even when the ropes pulled it to the ground, and the men slipped the metal reinforced collar around its neck and fastened chains to it.

They screwed another pole into the ground.

After they removed the ropes, the dog lay down and didn't move. The waiters who wanted to see it lash out at its new surroundings were disappointed. Even the man with the dark cheeks felt uneasy, though there was little chance of losing money. He could buy these shepherd dogs off the grasslands for a shockingly low price whenever he wanted. Tibet was full of good deals to be made if only you knew how. There was a rumor among the waiters that the boss had recently bought a piece of jade carved into the shape of an eggplant for just a couple of cans of gas and then had it escorted by two cars to Chengdu. No one knew how much he got for it, but it was a lot — let's put it that way.

The waiters left, their expectations dashed. Kelsang pulled on his chains and charged at the newcomer, barking, but the other mastiff ignored him. These days Kelsang found that once he started barking, he couldn't stop — at least not until he was overcome by sadness. But this time he felt none of the satisfaction he usually did, and so he calmed himself and lay down.

Toward evening, two waiters came with hind legs of mutton. The rusty red mastiff just lay where it was, not touching the meat that was thrown to it. Kelsang didn't understand why, but for the first time in his life he didn't feel like eating, either. He was too busy examining this new mastiff. The two waiters, so used to seeing Kelsang crunch his way through flesh and bone, were disappointed again and left, cursing.

The other mastiff really was getting old. Stiff brown hairs poked through its dull, faded red coat, and Kelsang could detect the smell of old age. Of all the smells he had stored up, it reminded him most of old leather. He didn't know what it was about this dog that fascinated him so much. Whenever the dog happened to look up, it seemed to gaze straight through him into the distance. This indifference made Kelsang panicky. Having been tied up for so long, he simply wasn't prepared to accept that he was to be ignored like this. He jumped up and pulled at his chains. But he didn't start barking — not because he couldn't, but because he didn't want to anymore.

Kelsang lay back down and followed the other mastiff's unmoving gaze. He himself regularly fell into such trances, but he would usually stare at the village at the foot of the mountain or at the restaurant glinting in the sunset with all the tour buses lined up outside. After staring like this for a while, some kind of mirage would appear — a summer pasture, the first snowfall of his memory, even the streets of Lhasa at night.

Every evening around this time, Kelsang would be woken from his thoughts by a clump of mud walloping against him, usually thrown by either the man with the dark cheeks or one of the waiters. Having spent the whole day bumping along Tibet's terrible roads, the busloads of tourists had eaten their fill, and reinvigorated by the heat of the chilis, were climbing up the hill to take a look at the huge furry monster tied up on the slope.

Kelsang's response would send the hushed crowd running, the sound of his clanging chains adding to the terrible noise coming from his throat. Only when they were farther away, where the restaurant owner guaranteed they would be safe, did they look back at Kelsang. This dog wanted nothing more than to chomp them to pieces, and they were too scared to get any closer. The tourists wasted no time snapping photos of the enormous dog as he tore around his pole, jumping up every now and again like one of Don Quixote's warring windmills. As soon as his paws hit the ground, he was ready to pounce again.

The man with the dark cheeks stood behind the crowd watching proudly. He was going to get his due. One day the wind would change, and that greedy smile would be stuck on his face. This was how business was done. The tourists would take their photos and videos home and show them to friends and family, spreading the word that in a village not far from Lhasa there was a fine mastiff for sale. Someone was bound to buy the dog for the price he wanted.

The rusty red mastiff continued to stare out toward the horizon, made fuzzy by the last of the evening sun, out past the endless gravel landscape to where clouds, swollen with rain, dotted the sky.

Kelsang couldn't see anything extraordinary.

By the third day, the other mastiff's meat had begun to give off a foul smell that put Kelsang off his food. He could only eat half of what he was given. The rusty red mastiff didn't even look at the meat, the fresh or the rotten. It just lay there, completely still. Occasionally, at night, it would get up and loop around its pole a few times, its chains dangling, before plopping back down on the ground with a thud. By the fifth day, its body was skin and bones, and it couldn't get up. Kelsang had never imagined that a mastiff could lose weight so quickly.

One of the waiters came with a bowl of milk, went

right up to the rusty red dog and placed it beside it. Kelsang watched as the mastiff looked up and stared into the distance, paying no attention to either the waiter or the milk.

On the eighth day, as evening drew near, the rusty red mastiff, now as thin as a piece of felt, tottered to its feet. This came as a shock to Kelsang. He smelled the reek of death in the wind. It was the same smell that had come from the dog shot on the streets of Lhasa. Kelsang hadn't seen a sign of life from the other mastiff all day. In fact, he thought it was already dead.

The rusty red mastiff hobbled a few steps, making no sound, as if its paws were padded. Then it leaned against the pole, its head weighed down by the chains, and a trickle of urine ran between its legs. It looked around dimly, as if making sure that everything was real, before lifting its head slightly to sniff the air. Capturing its last moments, it looked over at Kelsang.

And then it died.

Kelsang's wailing brought the people from the restaurant, but it was a different sort of wailing from the hopeless sounds he had been making in the past weeks and months.

Kelsang howled for an hour after they carried away the rusty red mastiff. Then he made a low sound, like the beating of a metal drum, and stopped abruptly.

The next day, the waiter arrived to discover that Kelsang hadn't touched the previous day's meat.

"What a mess!"

The man with the dark cheeks followed the waiter up the mountain to take a look at Kelsang and then rushed to the village to find a vet.

The medicine the vet prescribed was stuffed into his meat, but despite its alluring smell, Kelsang wouldn't touch it. He was tired and weak after all his wailing, and that feeling was scarier than hunger. He felt that everything in his life was slipping away. He had lost interest in all of it.

Kelsang was on a hunger strike.

On the third day, Kelsang tried to get to his feet, but he felt dizzy. If he went on like this, it wouldn't be long before he, too, would lie down never to get up again. But he wasn't destined to end his days in such a pathetic manner. His rescue was to come in the form of a yak.

Every evening at sunset, a herd of yaks was brought back from pasture to the village. That day, as the herd passed the Sichuan restaurant, one of the yaks suddenly charged into a *dzo*, an animal bred from a cow and a yak, jumping wildly, its fur flying. In a frenzy, it then began to gallop up the slope toward Kelsang.

The village's sheep and yaks sparked Kelsang's fading memories of summer out in the pastures, and recently he found himself staring at them even more than before. An urge would well up in him to steer them toward better grass, and he would stand up, eager to set off, until the sound of his clanking chains dragged his thoughts back to his barren mountainside and pole.

Perhaps the yak had been poked in the behind by a bull, or a fly flew up its nostril, or it was simply excited because it was mating season. Whatever the reason, it came stomping up the mountainside, creating a cloud of dust behind it like an armored truck.

Kelsang felt drowsy and was lying by his pole when he heard the sound of thundering hooves. He jumped to his feet. He couldn't figure out what this mad yak was after. Instinct told him to run toward it barking. That's what shepherd dogs do — round up animals who are straying from the herd.

The yak wasn't after anything in particular and was just trying to expend its energy before returning to the other animals. But Kelsang's barking had caught its attention, and without thinking, it started running toward the mastiff. Adult yaks weigh about half a ton, and so when running at full speed can't stop easily. Its eyes were red, and it was intent on bulldozing the mastiff into smithereens.

But Kelsang didn't cower. If it hadn't been for his chains, he would have long since powered himself forward. He knew that to turn this animal's giant weight against itself, all he had to do was whirl around and bite its hind leg. Then, as it turned, he could jump up and bite it on the other side. It wouldn't take long to exhaust the yak before sending it back to the herd, stunned and humbled.

But Kelsang was tied up, and aside from howling at the yak, he was powerless. He stretched and prepared to face the tank-like beast charging madly toward him. The yak didn't slow down. It was still determined to trample everything in its path.

Although Kelsang had a frighteningly massive frame, in the face of the crazed yak, even he looked rather feeble. He nimbly dodged to one side as the yak charged him, its half-moon horns lowered and ready to stab. As the yak continued forward, propelled by its own weight, Kelsang nipped behind and sank his teeth into a hind leg. This was the first time in ages that he had had something worth biting into. Without a moment's hesitation, he pushed his sharp teeth through the yak's fur and then quickly let go. He had caused enough pain to wake the yak from its trance. If he dug his teeth in any deeper, he might break its leg. This was a fundamental principle that all superior shepherd dogs understood — you don't break the leg of your master's animal.

In a cloud of dust, the yak passed Kelsang and crashed into the pole that had stood firm come rain or shine for months, snapping it like a matchstick under its hooves.

At first, Kelsang didn't understand the significance of what had happened. He had given up hope of getting his freedom back long ago. But as he pulled out of the yak's way, he felt his chains drop.

It had only taken an instant. The yak came to its senses as it crashed to the ground, the force of the impact against the pole making it lose its balance. It stood up, its face covered in dust, and panting heavily, tried to make sense of what had happened.

Kelsang had already lost interest in the yak and was running out onto grass yet to bear his footprints, beyond the circle permitted by his chains. The chains were still fastened around his neck, but he knew that he was free.

Dragging the chains behind him, Kelsang ran up the mountain slope in the direction where he and the rusty red mastiff had spent so long gazing.

Suddenly he encountered the man with the dark cheeks. He stopped, momentarily distracted. The man was even more shocked. He knew just how ferocious a mastiff could be after being tied up for a year.

Fear came crashing over him like a wave, and he slumped to the ground. He cupped his hands over his head and pulled himself into a tight ball. Perhaps it was more in self-defense than fear. He might look undignified, but at least the dog couldn't get at his neck and head. And so he lay perfectly still, like a pheasant chased into a snowdrift by a pack of hunting dogs.

But the man's attempt to play dead only confused Kelsang. He had never seen a human behave like this, and now that he finally had an opportunity to satisfy his desire to retaliate, he didn't know where to bite.

Of course, this was precisely why the man with the dark cheeks was lying on the ground tucked up like a human ball — so that the mastiff couldn't smell his pungent fear. In an instant, Kelsang lost his desire to attack. Maybe it was all to do with timing. If he had been given this chance shortly after being tied up, no doubt the man would have been torn to a pile of unsightly pieces.

A few of the waiters were running toward them shouting and carrying ropes and sticks. From a distance, it looked as if the dog had already mauled their boss, since he seemed to be a motionless pile of clothes on the ground.

"I told you from the beginning, that thing is no dog. Have you ever seen a dog like that?"

"What do you mean it's not a dog? A mastiff's not a dog?"

"Well, it's not a normal dog."

"I was getting water from the river when the boss told me to hurry up. He said he was going up the hill to pee. It could be me lying there on the ground."

The waiters spluttered about their close shaves as they ran up the mountainside, but they stopped a good distance from the dog. They stamped their feet and shouted, not wanting to get any closer.

Kelsang had already continued up the slope, dragging the chains behind him. He didn't feel that he absolutely had to return to the open grasslands, but he knew that was the direction he was heading.

Fearing that the dog had ripped open their boss's throat, the waiters approached cautiously. He was completely still, his bottom sticking up in the air. One of the waiters steeled himself and poked him with his stick.

Thinking the dog had taken his first bite, the man with the dark cheeks began to shake violently. But when he looked through the cracks between his fingers and saw only his waiters, he lifted his mud-caked face. He looked around to make sure that the dog had definitely gone and then struggled to his feet.

"What are you waiting for? Go after it!" he shouted.

There is nowhere to hide out on the open grasslands, no place to take temporary refuge. If the battered old truck hadn't broken down, spluttering like a cow that had been shot, who knows how long Kelsang would have been able to carry on.

A few times, the truck had come very close to driving over his chains, but the curves in the road prevented it from chasing him at full speed. Kelsang ran as fast as he could, his heart thumping a rapid drumbeat. It became harder and harder for him to catch his breath. At one point, darkness fell over his eyes, but only for a brief moment. He pressed on, the chains trailing behind him. He had been wearing these chains for more than a year now, and as he ran, his neck muscles grew even stronger with the strain. The pounds of metal had almost become a part of his body.

The waiters were standing in the back of the truck shouting. It only took ten minutes to catch up to the mastiff, but even then they didn't dare get too close in case they ran over the boss's treasure. So when they were close enough to chase him on foot, they poured down from the truck like a swarm of ants. But while they were arguing over who should grab Kelsang's chains, he took off and ran out of sight. They clambered back into the truck. After this happened a few times, Kelsang understood what was going on. As the truck approached, he would change direction, so that by the time it had turned around he was already out of reach.

Gradually, it grew dark. Kelsang was so tired he was panting violently, his tongue hanging out of his mouth. Fortunately, the truck made a sudden deafening cranking sound, as if it was about to fall apart, and spluttered to a halt.

Kelsang slipped away under the cover of darkness. As the waiters clambered down from the truck, they could hear the sound of chains bumping along the ground somewhere in the black night. Their boss was shouting and swearing, but they were all too scared to leave the broken-down truck and go in search of the dog.

Never again did Kelsang have to endure the sound of the voice belonging to the man with the dark cheeks.

It was now pitch black.

A fire of driftwood and yak dung. Two shadows that looked like flattened giants flickered as the flames danced in the gentle breeze, stretching out into the wilderness.

The two men were trying to put up a tent, but it wasn't going well. One was tugging from the outside while the other had climbed in. Suddenly the tent collapsed. Their laughter floated across the open landscape, but it was like the tiniest drop of water being sucked into a sponge, so vast was the silence of the wilderness.

When they finally got the tent to stand up on its own,

one of the men stood bolt upright, alarmed by the smell wafting toward them. With a shout, he ran to the fire and grabbed a pot. Hunger alone enabled him to withstand the burning hot metal before he dropped it on the ground, screaming and waving his hands. But he had managed to rescue the food, their only sustenance after driving all day across the grasslands.

"It doesn't look too burnt," said Han Ma, as he lifted the lid off the pot and sniffed.

"Yeah, but my hand is. Get the spoons in the jeep," said Yang Yan.

Finally, they sat outside their fully erected orange tent enjoying bowls of steaming hot meat congee. The stars were high in the night sky, and even though their stomachs were thundering with hunger, they paused to gaze up at the magical sight.

"The sky's different here. Look, Ursa Minor," Han Ma mumbled through a mouthful of congee.

"Is that the Little Bear? Where?" Yang Yan raised his head. "Yeah, it is different. A lot more stars, and it's so bright."

"Of course it's bright. We're more than thirteen thousand feet above sea level. We're much closer to the sky — we're on top of the world."

"Really?"

"This is the world's highest plateau…"

"Whatever. You've been talking about it the whole way. I'm not interested in your geography lessons," Yang Yan interrupted. "Show me the Little Bear instead."

"Over there. That really bright star is its tail." Han Ma pointed his spoon up at the vast sky.

"Where? Which one?"

"There."

"But the sky's full of stars!"

"Join up the brightest ones, and that's the Little Bear."

"Nonsense. How does that look like a bear? It's just a bunch of stars."

"Hmm, you have no imagination. Better stick to being a businessman."

"But I really can't see it." Yang Yan cocked his head, looking up.

Han Ma raised his arm, despite the ache in his shoulder from the day's drive, and tried to point out the constellation among the myriad stars in the sky.

"Do you have a weird feeling?" Han Ma asked, as he slowly lowered his arm.

"Like what?"

"Like someone's watching us."

Yang Yan's eyes widened. He moved closer to Han Ma.

"I just heard something," whispered Han Ma.

"Me, too. It sounded like metal clanging."

The two men fell silent, holding their breath and listening. But they couldn't hear anything. It was quiet — too quiet — they couldn't even hear the sound of a bird tweeting or an insect buzzing.

Han Ma finally broke the suffocating silence. "We're being too sensitive. It's nothing."

"Maybe we were wrong."

People often imagine that they hear things when they first come to the plateau. It's a symptom of altitude sickness. The tense atmosphere dissipated, and the two men began to give in to their exhaustion.

"Let's get the sleeping bags from the jeep."

But when Han Ma stood up, they heard the sound again, clearly this time. The two men froze, staring into the night. The sound was coming from the darkness close to their tent. Darkness is like an empty vessel waiting for humans to fill it with their imaginings. In only a few seconds, it had been magically transformed into a multitude of scary possibilities.

A minute passed, or maybe it was ten minutes. Yang Yan couldn't stand the silence any longer.

"Could it be a wolf?" he said, his mouth dry.

As if proving that this was a possibility, one they had summoned into existence by having the courage to speak it out loud, a sound of clanking metal came from the dark, followed by a hairy face.

Yang Yan spun around in fear and grabbed the knife in his backpack.

"It's a dog," Han Ma said, as his friend waved the knife in the direction of the still-indistinct shape, and clues started to appear. The animal's ears flopped down, and it was wearing a collar, so it had to be domesticated. It couldn't be a wolf.

The dog walked toward the fire. Its fur was a dusky gray, so covered in dust that it was difficult to tell its real color. Its eyes burned in the darkness, staring at them.

Maybe because of the knife in Yang Yan's hand, the dog growled but didn't come any closer.

"Put the knife away. You're scaring it."

Yang Yan had noticed how nervous the dog was. As soon as he tucked the knife away, it stopped growling, and its gaze moved straight to the pot full of congee.

"It must be hungry." Han Ma picked up the pot and edged forward slowly. The dusty gray dog took a few cautious steps back. Han Ma placed the pot on the ground and then stepped back himself.

"Do you think it'll eat it?" Yang Yan said from a few yards away.

"Probably."

The gray dog turned its head and gently sniffed the air, as if assessing the likelihood of danger. This slight movement revealed the source of the sound — the chains attached to its collar.

"It must belong to a herding family."

"But we haven't seen any camps all day."

"Maybe not, but this dog's domesticated. It can't just be wandering the grasslands by itself."

Kelsang concluded that there was no danger of being captured for the moment, so he walked toward the pot of congee, his chains dragging behind him. Then, covering the pot with his enormous head, he gulped it down. Han Ma and Yang Yan watched as the gray dog ate.

It had been two days since his escape, and Kelsang had been unable to find anything to eat. He continued running long after the truck broke down, only stopping in a shallow depression to sleep as the sun rose over the horizon. He woke around midday feeling very hungry. There had been one advantage to being tied up by the man with the dark cheeks. Every day like clockwork he'd been given a juicy chunk of fresh mutton. It had given him a voracious appetite that was now hard to satisfy.

Kelsang didn't know how far he'd run, but he was sure he was heading toward the open grasslands. He saw a bog in the distance where a few water birds were resting. Shepherd dogs aren't good at catching birds, but with hunger driving him forward, he pressed on. Before he made it to the water's edge, the birds took flight, screeching in alarm. All he could do was drink a few mouthfuls of the smelly water before carrying on. The chains were becoming a burden now, and even though the fur around his neck was especially thick, his muscles were constantly twitching with pain.

By the afternoon, Kelsang was so hungry that his legs were starting to give way. Then he came across a marmot. He ran after it with great care and attention until it escaped into a hole. He began digging. But the soil here was not as soft and crumbly as in his old pastures. It was full of small stones that lodged themselves in his paws. The sun had already begun to set by the time he finally dug down to the bottom of the burrow.

Perhaps hunger made him careless, because the marmot, who had been crouching at the bottom holding its breath, seized the opportunity to leap away. Kelsang was only one step behind, but the heavy chains around his neck prevented him from pouncing before the marmot jumped down a new hole.

The hole was not that small, but there was still no way Kelsang could fit into it. And there was no doubt that digging another hole was going to be a mammoth task when he was so tired. Frustrated, he turned and bit at the snake-like chains that were still attached to his collar.

Kelsang was almost mad with hunger and thirst when he heard the sound of a vehicle. At first he thought it was the man with the dark cheeks and his waiters, yet he didn't run away. His stomach was churning. He had to eat. Anyone wanting to capture him could have safely approached him now. He was hopelessly exhausted, and fury was beginning to burn inside his chest like a small but stubborn flame.

Kelsang pulled his chains up a slope. An unfamiliar-looking jeep stopped on the other side of the small hill. Two men, also unfamiliar, emerged from it and began collecting scraps of firewood.

Not long afterward, the sound of the two men talking drifted through the air from where they sat beside the fire. The aroma of meaty congee soon followed. To a dog who had spent so long away from human dwellings, the fire was irresistible. In ancient times, a group of wild animals had overcome their fear of fire, and this was how they had left the wilds and become man's companions. Fire, warmth, food, master. Irresistible fire.

Kelsang spent a long time looking around to make sure there was no sign of the man with the dark cheeks and his waiters. Then he began to creep closer to the heart of the flames.

By the time Kelsang finished licking the pot clean, Han Ma had already poured water into a jug, placed it before him and retreated. Kelsang hesitated a moment and then walked over and dipped his head into the jug. He drank calmly. The water was fresh, not like the stinky bog water.

"This dog's not bad. Why don't we keep him?" Yang Yan suggested. "He must be one of those mastiffs the locals talk about. They're good dogs."

"Someone will probably come looking for him tomorrow. They'll want him back." Han Ma was already inside the tent, unrolling his sleeping bag.

Before going to sleep, Yang Yan tried to approach the sleepy dog who had eaten and drunk his fill and was now lying in front of the jeep. He wanted to get hold of the other end of the chains. But while the dog may have looked drowsy, every time Yang Yan got close enough to pick up the chains, his half-shut eyes would flick open like a switch, shining a disquieting dark green light in his direction. A threatening growl followed that rumbled like a powerful motor, echoing in Yang Yan's ears. He could only withdraw his hand. Time and again the growl warned Yang Yan away until he eventually went back to the tent, defeated and drenched in sweat.

"That dog's too clever. There's no way to get close to him."

"Best not to touch him," Han Ma responded, looking up from his notebook. He was scribbling by the light of a headlamp.

"Maybe he'll leave in the night."

"Not necessarily. We'll see."

In the middle of the night, Han Ma and Yang Yan heard the rhythmic sound of heavy steps circling the tent, accompanied by the sound of chains trailing along the ground. They were tired, too tired to go out and see what was going on. The next morning they awoke to find Kelsang still there. The dog kept his distance as they stumbled out of the tent. He lay in the dewy grass some ten yards away, looking at them coldly.

By this time they were certain that he was a dog, of course. The collar and chains proved that. But who had ever seen a dog like this? With the long winter drawing to an end, Kelsang had begun to lose his heavy coat. The fur on his body had matted together like felt, making him look even larger than he really was — like a monster from the wilds.

After preparing a simple breakfast, Han Ma tried calling him.

Kelsang's hunger was not as fierce as the day before. He could feel that these two men were different from the man with the dark cheeks and his waiter helpers. They had stood watching as he ate but hadn't tried to force him to do anything. So that night, instead of running away, he had circled the tent, leaving his scent.

"He's coming over." Yang Yan watched in surprise as Kelsang stood up and walked toward them.

Kelsang stopped a few steps away from Han Ma. His smell was nothing like the sharp mixture of alcohol and cigarettes that came from the waiters. It was new and different. Kelsang was still keen on expanding his store of smells.

Han Ma was crouching down holding a sausage. But Kelsang had forgotten how to take food from a human hand. He hesitated. Should he teach this eager outstretched hand a lesson?

"Be careful. He could bite your whole hand off," Yang Yan warned.

"Shhh," said Han Ma, reaching out a bit farther.

Perhaps this movement overstepped some critical line for Kelsang, because he began to growl with his hair standing on end. He looked like a frightened seal baring its teeth.

"Be careful!" Once again, Yang Yan reached for the knife inside his bag.

"Don't move." Han Ma extended his hand farther still and opened it, exposing the sausage in his palm.

"I'm thinking this dog might have come from a nearby slaughterhouse. He doesn't trust you one bit," Yang Yan said, with a note of despair in his voice. He was waiting for Han Ma to start shrieking in pain.

There was some kind of force preventing Kelsang from ripping this man to shreds. He watched the two men closely. There was no way he was going to let either of them grab hold of his chains. He wasn't going to be tied up like that again.

It took forever to get Kelsang to eat the sausage. They'd already been on the road for an hour by this time the previous day. When Kelsang finally felt comfortable enough, he stepped forward and gently licked the sausage out of Han Ma's palm, letting it drop to the ground. His teeth made no contact with Han Ma's skin. Then he looked up, his hazy, dust-swept eyes finally showing some warmth. This was a pleasant surprise to Han Ma, who had been whispering to him the whole time. The dog's bush-like fur also began to settle back down.

Han Ma leaned farther toward Kelsang with an outstretched hand.

"Incredible," Yang Yan breathed, the sun piercing his eyes.

Han Ma's hand fell gently onto Kelsang's bristly mane, which looked and felt like dry autumn twigs.

Kelsang had not stopped growling, but even in that there was a subtle change, as its pitch undulated faintly with the movement of Han Ma's hand. He was so gentle, it was as if he was stroking a tiny seedling. As Han Ma's hand moved to his neck, Kelsang surprised himself by letting out a contented snort. It was as if he was back tucked under his mother's warm belly. He began to tremble uncontrollably. Not even Tenzin had ever stroked him there.

Han Ma felt Kelsang's matted winter coat and carefully began to pull at the loose tufts that should have fallen out, each one making a squeaking sound and puffing dust into the air. It was like excavating an object long-buried underground. Kelsang's old fur made a surprisingly large pile. Had it not been for this fur, he never would have survived the minus forty degree temperatures out on the exposed mountainside. The two men were amazed to discover such a magnificent dog underneath. His coat was a glossy blue black, so black that it shone. He was a rare beauty.

Han Ma began to tidy up the long fur that was caught under Kelsang's broken collar. The metal was digging into his skin, and the screws at the joints had rusted. Han Ma took the Swiss army knife from Yang Yan, but the glinting metal made Kelsang nervous. Han Ma soon discovered that all he had to do was stroke him gently, and the dog would calmly lower his head. Using the small saw, Han Ma began to cut through the metal wires in the collar as Kelsang whimpered in fear and pain. After about ten minutes of careful sawing, the collar fell away.

Kelsang didn't know what had happened until Han Ma stood up and flung the chains and collar on the ground. He shuffled back a few steps but didn't shake his head to check that they were really gone. In fact, through some sort of trick of the brain, he could still feel the weight of the cold, heavy chains around his neck. When he did finally move his neck, he was shocked to discover how much lighter it felt. He began to run clumsily toward the open grasslands. It had been so long since he had been able to run freely, and in no time he disappeared over a small hill.

"Gone," Yang Yan sighed, looking in the direction where Kelsang had vanished.

"So let him. But if he's always been chained up, he won't last long."

The two men packed up the tent, tidied up all their things and loaded the jeep. They looked out again at the grass glinting in the midday sun, but there was no sign of Kelsang.

They drove back toward the road. The only reason they had left it the night before was to find water, and now they were forced to keep stopping to make sure that they were retracing the tire marks in the grass. After about ten minutes, they managed to find their way back.

But just as they started to pick up speed, a black shadow ran in front of them, bringing the jeep to a screeching halt. Everything loosely packed inside fell out of place, and the two men nearly went crashing headfirst through the windshield.

There he was, the black mastiff, full of vitality as the wind blew through his coat. This was a completely different dog from the ferocious gray one in chains they had first met.

"He's come back!" Yang Yan said.

Kelsang didn't care that the jeep had nearly knocked him over. He stood confidently, his eyes just half open. He wasn't going to step aside.

"What does he want?" Yang Yan honked the horn twice, but the dog paid no attention and stayed just where he was.

"Maybe he wants to come with us." Han Ma got out of the jeep and opened the back door.

Kelsang walked around, hopped in and settled on top of the tent in the back seat.

Yang Yan pulled up at a restaurant in a small town for lunch. Kelsang woke from his deep sleep — he hadn't budged the whole way — jumped out and lay down in front of the jeep. All the other drivers in the restaurant gasped in admiration when they saw Kelsang. What a fine mastiff!

"Looks like we've got ourselves a guard," said Han Ma, leaving the door unlocked.

6
PROTECTING THE ANTELOPE

WHAT IS IT THAT ENABLES the antelope to survive the plateau's cruel winters? Beneath their thick fur is a layer of fur nearly seven times softer and more delicate than human hair and probably the world's finest and warmest. But it is precisely this fur that means the antelope can no longer live in peace the way they used to, or rather man's discovery of this fur has made it so. And now the entire species finds itself perilously close to extinction.

It didn't take humans long to realize that these skins, first used as modest coverings, could, in fact, be much more. The fur could be woven into robes embellished with precious stones, and then came cashmere coats and pashmina scarves. It was a magic material, as light as feathers. A shawl two yards long could be pulled through a wedding ring, and yet the making of it meant the sacrifice of three antelope. And if one of these antelope was a mother with young to feed, even more lives would pay for the garment. But it is just this kind of sumptuous, exclusive clothing that draws attention to its owner.

Every year more than twenty thousand antelope are killed, and many of those are calving mothers and their young. They are skinned, and their hides are sent to Nepal and India. The smugglers will risk life and limb for the six hundred percent profit they can make on one animal. Then in old workshops, skilled craftsmen take the blood-spattered skins and turn them into beautifully woven masterpieces to be sent off to the so-called civilized corners of the world. There they are sold for as much as twenty thousand dollars as luxurious accessories for glamorous women.

This bloody trade has devastated the antelope population. In 1900, there were some million antelope freely wandering the plateau. Nowadays reports say the number is less than seventy-five thousand.

A response has been mounted. Teams have started roaming the grasslands, protecting the antelope from poachers. Some of these idealistic people came together to form an environmental protection team under the supervision of the Tibetan Autonomous Region Committee for the Protection of Antelope.

They were known across the region as the guardian angels of the Tibetan antelope, and within two weeks of their meeting, Han Ma, Yang Yan and Kelsang became the newest members.

A couple of days after meeting Kelsang, Han Ma and

Yang Yan drove the cross-country jeep into the environmental protection station at Hoh Xil. As concerned environmentalists, they were donating the jeep to the cause.

The next day, Yang Yan and Han Ma became the first volunteers of the year to join the Antelope Protection Team's tour of the plateau mountains. They were driving the very same jeep, but it now had the team's name painted in red letters on the side. Two other members had joined them, so Kelsang had to be tied up in the narrow space between the rear windshield and the back seat.

Three vehicles drove into the grasslands of Hoh Xil. Stretching more than ten thousand miles across, they were almost empty of people and a paradise for wild animals. No one said much at first as they dealt with the effects of the altitude. The vehicles struggled up the mountains, much like the antelope. Now that the inspection had begun, one or two months of strenuous trekking lay before them, only to be interrupted by encounters with potentially violent poachers. Who knew what lay on the road ahead.

This was Han Ma and Yang Yan's first inspection. Until now, they had only read about them in newspapers or on websites, or seen programs about them on TV. They were overjoyed to finally be in the thick of the action. Unable to control their excitement, they began to sing all the songs they could remember, resorting to nursery rhymes once they had exhausted their adult repertoire. Kelsang growled in accompaniment, filling in the moments of silence when the two men were catching their breath.

"What do these guys do, exactly?" asked one of the men in the vehicle behind. "They have so much energy."

"Apparently one of them teaches kids with special needs and the other owns several large department stores. They've donated the jeep and thirty thousand *yuan*."

"Why have they got that dog with them?"

"They said they picked it up on the way."

"It's a nice dog."

During the first few days in Hoh Xil, the team was relaxed in a way they never had been before. They drove wherever they pleased across the virgin grasslands, without accident or breakdown to hold them up. As they drove farther in, they began to see wild donkeys. From a distance, these Tibetan donkeys looked very much like horses and could disappear with amazing speed, kicking up a cloud of dust.

It wasn't until the third evening, as the sun was setting, that they spotted their first antelope. They had just driven over a small hill when they saw them. The three antelope ran off in the opposite direction, their shadows sweeping across the landscape like clouds driven by a strong wind. For most humans it's a struggle to even walk at this altitude without shortness of breath and dizziness, yet these animals were remarkably graceful as they disappeared over a nearby hillock under the admiring gaze of the team.

But Kelsang was less interested in all this and didn't stare out the window anxiously like Yang Yan and Han Ma. He had seen antelope before, and these three animals awakened a memory in him — that was all. It had been well over a year since he had left his pastures, and he still couldn't fully comprehend all that had happened. These grasslands were more desolate than any he had lived on before, the spaces more open, with very few undulations in the topography. There was nothing between them and the distant horizon.

Kelsang still thought of his old pastures and his master, Tenzin, from time to time. It was like a reflex. He didn't need to make comparisons between his birthplace and the streets of Lhasa or the village with the restaurant. Before he had used running to satisfy his hunger for company, but now he had exactly what he had been longing for — a master.

This young man, Han Ma — who had pulled off his old winter fur, who had undone his chains — this was his new master. There is no way of knowing when wolves first began to live with humans, but from that moment on, they took a separate path from all other wild animals. No doubt they sometimes wanted to return to the wild, but what they really needed was a master — someone they could invest all their love and loyalty in, a human soul to whom they could belong.

The moment a dog develops this feeling, it lasts their whole life. Kelsang wouldn't let Han Ma out of his sight. Bumping along in the back of the jeep was deeply uncomfortable, but as long as he was with Han Ma, he was happy. He only allowed himself the luxury of sleeping after regularly checking that Han Ma was still in the front, gazing out at the landscape with a look of excitement on his face.

He mustn't, he simply couldn't, lose this master. Han Ma had been sent to him from heaven.

After choosing the location for that day's campsite, Han Ma opened the jeep door and Kelsang bounded out. He circled Han Ma's feet and then took off across the grasslands like a cheetah on the African plains at sunset, the landscape rising and falling like the folds of a giant's clothing, his glossy black fur fluttering in the wind. Most of the Antelope Protection Team were Tibetan, and some had been herdsmen, so naturally they understood the mastiff's value. They watched as Kelsang sped off toward the horizon only to return again at the same speed before rushing up to Han Ma, who was putting up his tent.

Kelsang carefully placed his front paws on Han Ma's lower back, slowing the force of the momentum that had been carrying him forward. He knew that this amount of pressure would make Han Ma lose his balance and fall over without hurting him. He did this after some consideration, even though he didn't know what would happen next. Somehow he couldn't control himself. Love burned inside him, and he couldn't stop it. Kelsang's previous decisions had come from instinct or the wisdom of accumulated experience, but this time it was emotion driving him. Love. For this man.

Han Ma fell on top of the tent, collapsing it. Yang Yan, who was holding the other end, watched in surprise. Kelsang waited. He had no idea how his new master would react once he picked himself off the ground. If he shouted or told him to get lost, that would be the end for Kelsang.

Han Ma's first thought was that one of the team had pushed him, but Yang Yan was standing in front of him, and the others didn't know him well enough for this kind of prank. They didn't seem the type, anyway.

He sat up in surprise and turned around. Kelsang was standing behind him with a look of expectation and a hint of confused puppy underneath his usual sleepy gaze.

The silence only lasted about a second before Han Ma started howling with laughter. He lunged toward Kelsang, threw his arms around his neck and dragged him to the ground.

Sunlight, the greenest grass, the warmest wind.

A new world opened up to Kelsang. Laughter, he understood. Humans only made this bright, rhythmic sound when they were happy. Whenever he had heard laughter out in the pastures, it meant that he was about to be given a piece of meat. But it was different this time. He couldn't control the wave of emotion that made him tremble all over. He had never felt like this before.

He barked in excitement, spinning around and throwing Han Ma off him. He jumped away before pouncing back on Han Ma as if he were a snow leopard or a wolf.

Yang Yan thought the dog had gone mad, and unsure what to do, he started shouting. The other members of the team had already taken their guns out of their backpacks.

But Han Ma wasn't frightened.

Kelsang pretended to bite Han Ma's hand, as if about to crunch through flesh and bone, but he just held the hand in his mouth. Underneath his mess of fur, his eyes were as calm as a lake warmed by the evening sun.

And so man and mastiff rolled around on top of the tent. Kelsang untangled himself and leapt to one side before jumping back on top of Han Ma. The spectators quickly understood that it was a game, and after a while, they went about their own tasks — lighting the fire, making dinner, fixing the jeeps rattled by the lack of road, putting up their tents.

"I thought you were being hurt!" Yang Yan exclaimed, as he grabbed one of the tent ropes.

"Stop!" said Han Ma, freezing like a basketball player in mid-dribble.

Kelsang stopped and lay down, panting. The look of pure joy was still in his eyes.

Playing like this was a completely new way for him to show his emotions. He had sort of played with Tenzin's son, but only out of loyalty to his master. The boy had really just been another duty around the camp. He was like a lamb, and playing with him was no different from looking after the flock. But with Han Ma it was different.

"He looks at you with such loving devotion. It's unbearable!" Yang Yan said.

After he finished putting up the tent, Han Ma changed the bandage he had put on Kelsang's neck. The wound caused by the metal collar was healing nicely. A feeling of pure happiness enveloped Kelsang. Feeling completely relaxed, he lay down beside Han Ma, whimpering like a puppy.

The tussling game became an important ritual each day when they stopped to set up camp. One day the convoy came to an impassable section of road, and each car broke down, one after the other. The team members got out and began pushing their vehicles, taking on an armor of thick mud in the process. They were exhausted by the time they reached the campsite, and Han Ma could only think of crawling into his sleeping bag. But he could see the familiar glimmer in Kelsang's eyes. He was waiting to play their game.

Han Ma decided he would stay in the jeep until dinnertime, but Kelsang waited patiently outside the door. Eventually, Han Ma had no choice but to get out, and even though he could barely walk, he summoned the last of his energy to tumble with Kelsang, sending the other team members into fits of laughter.

Kelsang had embarked on an entirely new life.

He wasn't exactly sure what it was the humans were doing, but as they pushed deeper and deeper into the wilderness, he could see that everyone, including his master, was becoming increasingly anxious. Their eyes were constantly fixed on the horizon. They were clearly looking for something, but all signs of life seemed to have vanished. Apart from the wild donkeys and the three antelope they had spotted in the first few days, they had seen nothing. There was only the monotony of the grass for as far as the eye could see, varying only slightly with the undulating topography, and the bright blue of the sky that hurt your eyes when you stared at it for too long.

But Kelsang didn't feel anxious. He had adjusted remarkably quickly to being tied up outside the village, and now that he had Han Ma, he was happy and didn't expect much more from life.

He was almost obsessed with his new master. Every evening after dinner, Kelsang watched as Han Ma picked up some sort of machine and walked away from the campsite. Han Ma would look all around him before raising the machine to his face. A crisp clicking sound would follow, then his master would look up, contented and relaxed as he gazed into the distance again. Kelsang had already developed a respect for man's machines, and the fact that this one was in Han Ma's hands made it even more important.

Then one day Han Ma aimed his machine at Kelsang.

"Okay, don't move," he said.

Kelsang struck his best pose, full of vigor.

After the now-familiar click sounded, Han Ma smiled and walked over to Kelsang, giving him an affectionate stroke on the head.

"Nice pose."

From then on, Kelsang waited patiently every day for Han Ma to point his machine at him after his walk. This must be some sort of reward or way of showing trust, he thought. But Han Ma never did point his machine at Kelsang again. It was a great disappointment to him, and even though he couldn't see his master pointing his machine at anything else in particular, a feeling of jealousy gripped hold of him.

It was early morning, and they hadn't been on the road for long. Kelsang suddenly felt a change in the atmosphere when the man in the police hat called out, and everyone's eyes lit up. Then, aside from the rumbling of the engine, there was silence. Everyone was transfixed by the view up ahead.

Kelsang couldn't help but be affected by the atmosphere. He could tell that whatever they had been waiting for had just happened.

The three vehicles drove into a small valley, and since there was no road ahead, everyone climbed out of their cars and proceeded on foot. The team leader warned Han Ma that it was vital that no one make a sound, so Kelsang was tied up inside the jeep.

The team members knew exactly what to do. They took their guns and started climbing up one side of the valley. Han Ma and Yang Yan followed. Han Ma was carrying half an antelope horn that he had picked up, while Yang Yan held tightly to his Swiss army knife.

Before long, Han Ma and Yang Yan were lagging behind the rest of the group. As they clambered to the top,
they heard a shot and rushed forward. Han Ma was so
tired, a black cloud seemed to descend over his eyes, but
when he looked over the hill, he managed to make out
two parked cars and five people scattering in different
directions.

"Do we follow them?" Yang Yan panted, catching up
to the rest of the team.

"Yes!" replied Han Ma, already running.

They thought at first that the poachers had been too
nervous to start their cars, but later they discovered that
one of their vehicles had broken down. The poachers
had no idea where to go and seemed to have forgotten
that there was no point in trying to run anywhere in this
vast open landscape.

Han Ma and Yang Yan chased a young man in a black
down jacket to the edge of a large crevice, a topographi-
cal scar from when the plateau had formed thousands of
years ago. In global terms, it was a mere wrinkle on the
earth's surface, but at over ten yards wide, it was too far
for the poacher to jump across.

The young man may have had a bad leg, otherwise it's
unlikely that Han Ma and Yang Yan could have reached
him so quickly. They stumbled up to him, their eyes
misted over from lack of oxygen and their hearts thumping so hard it felt like they would leap from their chests.

Having reached the dead end at the edge of the crevice, the young man turned around revealing his dark,

weather-beaten face. He was holding something above his head.

"A gun!" Yan Ya exclaimed. He was farther behind, yet he saw it before Han Ma.

Han Ma didn't hear him, and within moments the barrel of the gun was only inches from his head. He froze, his eyes fixed on its gaping black mouth.

The young man's face twisted in distress like a cornered leopard.

The crack of a shot.

In that moment, Han Ma thought it was over, but the bullet scraped past his shoulder. By the time he came to his senses, Kelsang's teeth were firmly planted in the poacher's wrist. He had brought the man to the ground and was now towering over him. His furious barks sounded like bones snapping, one after the other.

Yang Yan grabbed hold of Kelsang's head, while Han Ma forced his jaws open in an attempt to save the poacher's bloody hand. The man groaned.

"He nearly bit through it." Yang Yan examined the ugly face before him. "But did you see how that bullet scraped past your shoulder?" he said, turning to Han Ma. "Feathers flew out of your jacket! If the dog hadn't pounced on him, that bullet would've gone right through you." He picked the gun off the ground.

"I'll tie him up," Han Ma said, trying to calm Kelsang, who was still trembling with anger.

Kelsang shook the long fur on his neck and stared at the terrified poacher with deathly cold eyes.

"Haven't you noticed the rope's broken?" said Yang Yan. "A rope can't hold that dog."

The chewed-through rope dangled from Kelsang's neck.

The truth was that when Han Ma left with the others, Kelsang had felt abandoned. He hadn't let Han Ma out of his sight in days, and even at night, he lay in front of his tent and wouldn't let anyone near. It hadn't taken much to bite through the rope and squeeze through the half-open window of the jeep. He had started running in the direction of the hill the instant his paws touched the grass.

Kelsang had been greeted at the top by absolute chaos, but it still didn't take him long to spot Han Ma. He ran over just in time to see the poacher raise the gun to his master's head. He didn't understand what was happening, but he had experience with guns. The sound of the dying dog's cries on the street in Lhasa started echoing in his ears, and the fear of losing Han Ma flooded him. Without a thought to anything else, he rushed over to the two men, leapt into the air and lodged his teeth in the poacher's wrist, knocking the bullet off its intended course.

The other team members joined them after they had caught the remaining poachers. The scene before them made their eyes pop, and the team leader breathed a deep sigh of relief once he was sure that neither of the volunteers had been hurt.

Kelsang, for his part, wouldn't take his burning red

eyes off the poacher, who was now being led away. He even tried to wriggle free from Han Ma to have another go.

"That was close. The poacher nearly got you!" The team leader looked admiringly at Kelsang. "What an excellent dog. We need a mascot like him!"

But Kelsang didn't become a mascot for the team. A week later, Kelsang, Yang Yan and Han Ma left Hoh Xil so that they could take the tired jeep to be fixed in Golmud. It needed a complete overhaul after the tough driving conditions on the grasslands. This was to be their last assignment as volunteers for the Antelope Protection Team.

7

HEADING NORTH

ALL DAY THE JEEP lurched along the dirt road that had been torn up by heavy rain, and yet they only managed to cover around sixty miles. Rivers of mud had destroyed parts of the route, and at times they had to edge around piles of stones, mindful of the fact that not five yards to the right or left was a drop to a deep valley strewn with car wrecks. It was so nerve-racking that Han Ma and Yang Yan took turns driving every five miles, each one taking his place in the passenger seat drenched in sweat.

Kelsang was sitting up in the backseat. Every time they went over a hole in the road, he was flung to the side, and the terrible sound of the chassis scraping against stones echoed in their ears. As the engine gasped for life, he would climb back into a sitting position.

But the dangers of the road didn't dampen the two young men's enthusiasm, and whenever they got stuck behind other vehicles, they would chatter about the adventures ahead. Gripped by excitement at one point,

Yang Yan leaned back and stroked Kelsang on the head. But he was met with an angry growl, and seeing Kelsang's sharp teeth, he whipped his hand back.

"He won't bite. He's just warning you, that's all," Han Ma laughed, as he patted down the fur on the back of Kelsang's neck.

But the scare brought Yang Yan down to earth. Even though they'd spent two exciting weeks with Kelsang, he wasn't like an ordinary pet who developed affection freely and easily.

"Do you think he's part wolf? said Yang Yan. "They can never be tamed. Think about it. Circuses have tigers, lions, even, but have you ever heard of a tame wolf? No. And do you know why? Because they just can't be tamed. I've been feeding cans of beef to a wolf!" He drew farther back.

"Of course, he's not a wolf," Han Ma replied. "He's a dog, and you'll never find one as good as him. Look at him. He's trying his best to let us be his masters."

"He doesn't want me for a master. You're the one he's chosen." Yang Yan reached for the water.

Han Ma carefully parted the fur around Kelsang's neck and examined his wound. It had recovered completely.

Kelsang sat quietly, letting Han Ma stroke his neck.

Ever since meeting Han Ma, his life had changed. Having Han Ma for a master was completely different from living with Tenzin or the old painter. (He had never considered the man with the dark cheeks his master. He had tied him up for a year and hadn't looked after him.) Sometimes he felt as if he was part of Han Ma and Yang Yan's gang. Something welled up inside him every time Han Ma called him or stroked him, and the emotion surprised him. It was love.

As evening approached, the jeep crawled like a heavy tank into the parking lot of a small wooden guesthouse tucked under a cliff by the side of the road. They would eat here and spend the night. Han Ma and Yang Yan had slept in a tent ever since leaving Hoh Xil and were extremely happy to have found the guesthouse.

After they went inside, Kelsang jumped down from the jeep and lay in front of it, as he did every night. No one who had spent days driving on these exhausting, purgatorial roads had the energy to covet other people's belongings, but Kelsang was used to keeping guard. It was his new job. No one could get close to the jeep. It belonged to his master, and he was protecting it.

By the time Kelsang finished the water and steamed buns Master brought out to him, the sky was dark and the lights in the guesthouse had gone out, one by one. The guests were eager to sleep after bumping along such a washboard of a road all day. Kelsang was tired, too, but as he curled up with his head tucked close to his belly, something began to disturb him. His eardrums were hurting.

He looked up toward the guesthouse in the inky darkness. All was quiet except for the sounds of snoring and of someone muttering in their sleep. And yet a maddening feeling was growing inside him to the point that he could hardly bear the pressure. Then it slowly dawned on him that it was not madness, but fear. A creeping fear was pressing on his chest.

Kelsang froze, trying to detect the sound of Han Ma among all the other snoring guests. It was impossible. There were too many sounds drowning him out.

Fear closed in on Kelsang, restricting his breathing. It wasn't his experience on the grasslands that was telling him something was wrong, but pure animal instinct. The feeling passed quickly, yet it threw him into confusion, disrupting his rest. Perhaps it had just been some small change in the air or a faint noise. Kelsang couldn't make sense of it. It reminded him of the feeling he'd had one snowy winter day when he'd started barking and circling the yurt and had finally resorted to banging against it when he received no response. Luckily, Tenzin realized that something must be wrong, and just as the family stepped outside, the felt tent collapsed from all the snow piled on top.

It had been a strange omen and showed that Kelsang was particularly sensitive to danger. And something told him that the danger was even greater tonight.

By the time Kelsang's crazed barking awoke Han Ma, the dog had taken action. First he ran around the guesthouse barking as loudly as he could. When the people inside ignored him, he started ramming into the wooden door, and after a few knocks it flew open. It took Kelsang less than a second to find Han Ma.

The guesthouse was only open for business half the year, when the roads were passable. There were just two rooms — one at the front, with a wide platform bed and a couple of wooden tables, and a kitchen at the back. All the guests along with the people working in the guesthouse slept on the bed.

The employees, who were never as exhausted and didn't sleep as deeply as most of the guests, were already awake. They had just had time to get up and light the storm lanterns when the black shadow came crashing through the splintered wood, clambered over the sleeping guests and jumped on Han Ma. Han Ma awoke to find the others staring at the huge dog from under their covers. He was barking so loudly the room shook.

Han Ma had no idea what was going on, and he wasn't happy to have been pulled from his nice, cozy dreams in such a fashion. But he knew something must be very wrong from the way Kelsang was pulling desperately at his sleeve. He had never seen the mastiff so crazy before.

"If it's not too much trouble, can you get it to shut up? Maybe take it outside or something," a sleepy truck driver complained.

Apologizing, Han Ma put on his shoes and was pulled outside through the broken door by Kelsang's tight grip on his sleeve.

"Buddy, you're paying for that door," one of the employees called from inside.

"It's probably got rabies," muttered another driver. No one had managed to sleep through the racket. It was going to be an exhausting night.

Kelsang pulled Han Ma all the way to the jeep before letting go, but he wasn't planning on calming down just yet. He started running, jumping and barking.

Han Ma couldn't see anything unusual. The sky was clear after the day's heavy rain, and the Milky Way shone like a celestial river. The air was eerily still. There were no signs that the jeep had been broken into, and there were no strangers about.

Puzzled, Han Ma stared at Kelsang.

Suddenly Kelsang stopped barking. The sound continued to echo in Han Ma's ears as he followed the direction of the dog's gaze. Up on the cliff above the guesthouse, the root of a tree swayed in the moonlight as if being blown by a gentle wind. But the night was perfectly still.

A sound like gurgling water.

"Landslide!" Han Ma shouted.

He ran back inside the guesthouse, jumped up onto the bed and began to kick Yang Yan, who was still asleep. Then he kicked the other guests. Han Ma's shouts were followed by curses, and the midnight quiet turned into the clamor of an air raid as everyone tumbled out of the building in their nightclothes. Kelsang followed, marshalling them like a flock of sheep scattered by a violent snowstorm. Using his head, he pushed against the last driver's pudgy bottom, as he waddled, penguin-like, outside.

They didn't understand what was going on, but they knew it was bad. This crazy dog and his equally crazy master were determined to have them out of their sweet dreams and into the crisp night air at any cost.

Nine people stood in the parking lot. Those who had not had time to put on their shoes cursed as they hopped on the freezing concrete. They were shocked by the ferociousness of the dog, who was now standing beside Han Ma, and were careful not to make any sudden movements. One careless move and that dog would be on you, they were sure of it. It would rip you to shreds.

Han Ma couldn't hear anything over the confused questions, and he began to wonder if he might have been wrong.

"You're not sleepwalking, are you?" Yang Yan asked, rubbing his eyes from where he crouched on the ground. Despite the mad rush, he hadn't forgotten his sleeping bag and was wrapped up inside it.

Before Han Ma had time to answer, the cliff did it for him. A crashing that sounded like the sky falling in echoed all around them. It was like water blasting through a riverbank and was followed by the creaking of a tree falling over and then another deafening crash.

By the time it had all gone quiet again, the guesthouse, a place that had seen so many sweet slumbers, had disappeared, along with half the cliff that had once towered above it. Over ten thousand tons of rock and gravel had buried the place where they had been sleeping only moments ago.

Han Ma only lost a sleeping bag.

"Buddy, no need to pay for that door," said the guest-house worker.

Over the next few days, Kelsang enjoyed many cans of meat given to him as gifts — eighteen cans of meat, from four drivers and three guesthouse staff, to be precise.

Han Ma and Yang Yan were finishing up the handover of the jeep in Golmud. Han Ma had tied Kelsang to a tree in the courtyard before going inside to make arrangements. As he waited, Kelsang discovered that he had the ability to predict his own future. He watched Han Ma's every move — the handshake, the goodbye. And then they left without even glancing his way. Kelsang was confused. It wasn't possible. This was the very thing he had always worried about.

The noise of traffic drowned out the sound of Kelsang's barking before Han Ma and Yang Yan even reached the street.

"Are you still thinking about that dog? I doubt he's missing us," Yang Yan said, walking ahead with his back-pack.

"Hmm," Han Ma replied. He quickened his pace, even though it was a while before the train would leave.

They crossed two roads in silence before turning into a busy street lined with stalls of roasting meat. The air was thick with smoke from the coals. Gradually, they be-gan to notice that there was something different about

the way everyone was looking at them. It was the very
fact that everyone was looking at them that made them
uneasy. At first they thought it was because of the way
they were dressed. They were still wearing their expedi-
tion gear. But that seemed unlikely since this was the
only route into Lhasa, and there were hikers everywhere
with huge backpacks. The people of Golmud must be
used to it.

Slowly they realized that people weren't looking at
them, but at something behind them.

Han Ma turned around. "The dog!" he exclaimed.

It was indeed Kelsang standing behind them, a rope
trailing from his neck with a large tree trunk attached to
it. He was silent apart from his violent panting, his rib
cage rising and falling as he recovered from running to
catch up to them. He looked intently at Han Ma, searching his eyes for answers.

When Han Ma had disappeared, Kelsang's first reaction had been to bark madly in confusion. Then he suddenly stopped and put his energy into pulling on his
rope instead. He pulled and pulled, and each time the
tree shook, scattering a carpet of leaves on the ground
but nothing more.

For the people standing in their doorways, it was like
watching a machine performing a mechanical movement over and over again. But Kelsang wasn't paying any
attention to his surroundings. He was just stubbornly
trying to break the rope so that he could find Han Ma.
The onlookers sensed his urgency, and someone even

tried to approach to untie the rope. He couldn't bear to see the dog struggling. But the others stopped him. It would be dangerous to get too close.

When the tree finally came down — this time the rope was stronger than the tree — Kelsang nearly fell over, but he didn't pause for more than a second before running straight out of the courtyard.

The crowd let out a sigh of relief, and some people even looked happy.

Kelsang took no notice. He was too busy desperately searching for Han Ma's scent. As soon as he found it, he began to gallop. A couple of times, he feared he had lost the trail, but in his momentary despair he always found his lifeline again — the tiniest trace of Han Ma.

He bumped and crashed his way through a crowd of people, who parted, screaming.

An enormous dog dragging a tree trunk with a rope around its neck was running through the streets of Golmud.

Finally, Kelsang caught sight of Han Ma's familiar shape and became calm. He tried to draw up behind him casually, as if nothing had happened.

"Come here," Han Ma said.

Kelsang walked over to him and nuzzled his hot head against Han Ma's chest, sticking out his dry tongue to lick his hand. This was Kelsang's world now. He started whimpering and trembling uncontrollably, just like a little puppy.

"Look, it's not that big a deal," Yang Yan said. "Mastiffs

can be shipped by train. Let's go. We have time to make the arrangements before we leave." He wasn't used to being the center of attention and was getting nervous. A crowd had gathered, many of them chewing on Golmud's famous meat kebabs as they watched to see what was going on.

Han Ma and Yang Yan rushed off in the direction of the train station with Kelsang in tow.

"You didn't choose a spindly tree on purpose, did you?"

"Um...no, of course not," Han Ma replied.

They boarded the train at Golmud.

Han Ma put Kelsang in a cage that was then lifted into the baggage car. Instinct told Kelsang to refuse to be put into this narrow space with barely enough room to turn around, yet something else told him to trust his master. He knew he was leaving the plateau, but his life on the grasslands was already so far behind him. The strange thing was he didn't feel afraid or even sentimental. He trusted Han Ma. This young man was more important to him than the plateau.

Kelsang patiently lay down in his cage. The door closed, and the baggage car was plunged into darkness. He didn't see Han Ma for the rest of the journey.

The attendant who came to feed Kelsang was terrified that he might break out of the cage and maul him. Each time he would slide the food and water through a narrow hatch before turning and running, locking the baggage car door as quickly as he could.

Kelsang could only tell when day turned to night and back again by the light that came through the crack under the door. His sense of smell was sharper in the dark, picking up on anything that made it through the crack. He could tell when they were passing a lake, or maybe a forest, by the smell of dampness that greeted his nose. He was especially excited when they pulled into a station, and a whole mix of new and strange smells invaded the baggage car. Each one was cross-referenced against his bank of known scents, providing him with enough entertainment to last for hours once the train was on the move again. He couldn't see the world outside his car, but he knew that it was unusually rich in smells.

They had to change trains twice. People streamed through the crowded platforms, and even though everyone was busy trying to find their train, a glimpse of Kelsang was enough to elicit excited gasps. The passengers would find their seats, stow their luggage, then turn to the other passengers, exclaiming, "I just saw the most enormous dog!" Many journeys over those few days were spent discussing the fine black animal in the cage.

As evening approached, Kelsang entered a dream world where he could return to the pastures of his birth. Once he felt as if he was really clambering to the top of a pile of fleeces, his paws sinking into the softness, until he could keep his balance no longer and tumbled to the ground.

Suddenly a dazzling beam of light flicked across the

baggage car. An even larger cage was carried in and placed beside Kelsang's. This is how the nightmare began.

As the first rays of morning light shone through the crack at the bottom of the door, Kelsang saw that the cage beside him contained seven small dogs of a kind he had never seen before. They were slender, with short white fur, so short that the pink of their skin shimmered beneath it, and it was embellished with an even spattering of black spots. Their crystalline black eyes blinked at him, each pair matching the black spots, so that he had to look extremely carefully to distinguish between the two.

Of course, Kelsang couldn't know that ever since the release of *101 Dalmations* people had become obsessed with these cute dogs and had discovered that they made perfect pets. Their value had rocketed accordingly, and so it was that these seven puppies had one day found themselves caged and put on a train on its way to the city, where they would be sold.

But Kelsang didn't give a hoot for these dogs.

Then the puppies began barking. It started with just one of them. Perhaps the cage was too crowded, and one puppy had stepped on another. Or maybe one had been on the receiving end of some misdeed by one of its identical friends, like having its face pressed up against the bars. The others were then somehow infected and began wailing in distress, the sound escalating within moments to a full-blown puppy chorus that filled the baggage car.

Once it started, it didn't stop. The puppies were yelping and wailing. They were so loud that as the train passed through stations along the way, people waiting on the platforms could almost imagine that the dogs inside were having a drunken New Year's party. The puppies had first staged this performance when the door closed on them, and they were left in the dark. Kelsang managed to shut them up, at least temporarily, with a few fierce barks, only to discover seven pairs of fearful eyes staring back at him.

That was the end of Kelsang's authority. After that, no matter how much he barked or crashed against the sides of his cage, the puppies continued to wail. This was an unimaginable torment. Their emotional state was infectious, and he, too, started to find the never-ending darkness unbearable. He began to hate his cage and started thudding against it, walloping against the bars that bore traces of the scents of other animals.

Luckily, he only had to spend a day in the company of the black-and-white spotty dogs. Before they knew it, they arrived at the last stop — Harbin. It was just as well. If the journey had been any longer, Kelsang would have gone mad.

After emerging from the baggage car, Kelsang's excitement to see Han Ma was instantly dampened by what he saw around him. The station was full of people — men, women and children — people with all different smells. Of course, Han Ma and Yang Yan would have preferred to see the wilds of Hoh Xil bustling with antelope.

Kelsang had never in his life seen so many people. The variety of smells made him feel dizzy. He wanted nothing more than to press himself up against his master, and Han Ma tightened his rope. Having Han Ma with him dispelled his desire to bite and tear everything around him.

Kelsang had grown up near the snow-capped mountains of the Tibetan plateau in landscapes that could only be described as imposing and magnificent. But now, looking out at a completely manmade environment, he couldn't help but feel respect. Buildings encased in glass reached up into the sky, their shiny blue skins reflecting its color in the evening sun, just like the snowy peaks. This was the only part of what lay before him that made him feel at home.

"He's probably the first Tibetan mastiff ever to have made it to Harbin, wouldn't you say?" Yang Yan said, lugging his huge backpack.

"Probably," Han Ma replied.

They threaded their way through the crowds on their way out of the station. How Kelsang would react to all the people thronging at the exit like huddled sheep was anyone's guess.

Kelsang had come to a conclusion while sitting in his cage on the train. A large, energetic dog like him needed plenty of space. Luckily, Yang Yan's family lived in a villa with a huge lawn that the two men believed would make a perfect new home for him.

8

LIFE WITHOUT HAN MA

AFTER THE TIRING journey, Kelsang was pleased to find that the villa was situated on a large stretch of grass. As soon as his paws touched the soft green carpet, a spasm of pleasure shot through his legs. This was the real stuff — hot mud full of life — so different from the dusty rubber floor of the baggage car. Perhaps because he was distracted, or perhaps just because he was tired, he did not resist when Yang Yan replaced his collar and attached a new set of chains to it. And so it was that Kelsang moved into a luxury residential estate on the banks of the Songhua River in Harbin.

Kelsang sniffed at his kennel and detected the faint trace of another dog. It was all so new and strange. He stared at the long bridge that lay across the river. Since getting off the train at Harbin, he had seen things he never would have encountered had he stayed on the grasslands. On the first day, a train whistled across the bridge, and Kelsang ran toward it, barking. He had seen trains before, of course, but they had been stationary when he had been loaded in and out of baggage cars, and as far as he was concerned, he had essentially been housed in a series of storage rooms.

Yang Yan laughed at Kelsang's childishness. But it only happened once. By the time the second train passed less than an hour later, he merely looked up from where he lay in front of his kennel. Trains were nothing special now.

"Hmm... never thought you'd get used to things so quickly," Yang Yan said, thinking out loud.

But when the sun set, something happened that Kelsang couldn't have imagined in his wildest dreams. A steamship whistle blew into the silence. Kelsang exploded at the sight of the long, narrow object on the river and watched nervously as it went by, its decks filled with people looking out at the scenery. From the corner of his eye, he caught sight of Yang Yan standing on the balcony, and so he suppressed his instinct to howl — the only way he knew how to express his curiosity, fear and confusion.

The boat and the train were both large and noisy. Everything was so much more complicated than up on the plateau, and he was struggling to process it all. He watched attentively as the boat spurted steam across the surface of the water, now painted a bright red by the setting sun.

Kelsang was adapting well. It was the only way he would survive. This was what enabled mastiffs to live on the Tibetan plateau, what made them able to cope with the lack of oxygen and become an integral part of the grasslands.

Kelsang's life was once again full of firsts — the first time he saw a bicycle outside the gate, his first bus, his first plane. The air was full of new smells, which took a lot of effort to categorize and store, and which he wasn't always successful in placing. He tried to connect all these new experiences with Yang Yan, who had brought him here but now only seemed to appear when he drove his car into the garage at night. He tried to persuade himself that Yang Yan was now his master, and that he must obey this man who always came home with the strong, sharp smell of alcohol.

But Kelsang couldn't make himself respect Yang Yan enough, let alone love him the way he did Han Ma. Kelsang still thought of Han Ma, the young man who had tended his wounds. The concept of "master" had never felt so remote, not since he left the grasslands, and even when he had been with Tenzin, he hadn't really understood what it meant. He had only ever been playing the role that all shepherd dogs are supposed to. He hadn't needed Tenzin.

A week passed and still Han Ma didn't come. Kelsang began to wail in sorrow. Life had lost its meaning. All he did every day was lie in his kennel with the air-conditioning on and stare blankly at the cars that passed by every now and again. In the evenings, he paced, dragging his chains behind him. He drank, and he ate the finest imported dog food that money could buy.

Kelsang hadn't exactly gone mad, but he had taken

to barking at the empty street for over half an hour at a time. He fell into a simple, unchanging rhythm, so regular that it made people think they were listening to the turning cogs of a machine. For Kelsang, being trapped on these grounds was just like being tied up on the mountain. The only difference was that he now had an air-conditioned kennel that provided him with a cool breeze in the scorching heat.

Occasionally, Yang Yan would take Kelsang for a walk, but it was only so that he could show him off. The walks went no way toward satisfying Kelsang's desire to exercise. In order to get some relief, he'd pull on his chains and pounce on imaginary enemies. The green grass in front of his kennel was quickly torn up as though a horse had galloped over it.

When Kelsang went out with Yang Yan, he was shocked to discover that there were a great many dogs in the neighborhood. He couldn't imagine how they had possibly grown up here. Some of them looked like balls of fur. Others were sturdy, with extremely short hair. Kelsang was particularly intrigued by a Shar-Pei, its gray skin folded into deep wrinkles around its face as though it carried all the world's worries. Yang Yan pulled him past, but he still kept turning around to look at it, attempting to find its eyes hidden among the folds of skin.

Han Ma usually came to visit once a fortnight. These days were grand occasions, almost like holidays for Kelsang. He could detect Han Ma's footsteps from two hundred yards away, and he would leap out of his kennel in excitement and stand staring at the main gate. When Han Ma appeared, he would start jumping and yapping, and when he left, Kelsang wailed mournfully, already waiting for his return.

Kelsang was developing a real sense of time and somehow began to know instinctively when two weeks had passed. On days when Yang Yan found him spinning in circles in front of his kennel, looking up every now and then in the direction of the gate, he knew it must be Sunday — the day Han Ma was due to visit.

You could say that the reason Kelsang left the villa was because a dog shouldn't have such an accurate body clock. For some reason, three months after his arrival, there was a three-week period in which Han Ma didn't come. Kelsang thought he heard his master's footsteps a few times one week, but the repeated disappointment turned him to hysterical barking and made him violent. His teeth began to itch, so strong was his desire to bite into something. In fact, the desire to sink his teeth into hot flesh swallowed up everything else.

One evening, as the sky grew dark, Yang Yan took Kelsang for a walk. He didn't notice any particular change in the dog, who pulled at the leash as he always did. A successful young businessman was taking his mastiff to the local square and would then go back to his beautiful house. They walked around the patch of neatly trimmed grass in the square. Everything was as usual, right up until the sudden appearance of a Great Dane, that is.

Kelsang already knew about this dog. Sometimes, when he was barking on the lawn, he heard the sound of another dog barking along with him. It was a terrible bark, like someone striking a metal bucket with a stick. The noise alone told Kelsang that it came from an enormous dog.

The dog was indeed large, with black and white spots and pointy ears. It was being led by a plump man, who had obviously taken great care in raising it. Its long limbs raised it half a head above Kelsang. It was strong and arrogant, with a glossy coat.

The desire for a fight had been building up in Kelsang, yet he didn't much feel like stirring up trouble. The Great Dane slowed as it caught sight of him and stared suspiciously. As the distance between them narrowed, it tried to run at Kelsang, pulling tight on its studded leash.

The Great Dane had fought a German shepherd and a Doberman, winning each time, thanks to its considerable size. As if showing off, the plump man didn't pull on the leash, but loosened it instead. The Great Dane galloped up to Kelsang like a small horse and tore into his hind leg.

Tibetan mastiffs are particularly skilled at staying calm in an attack. Kelsang had already smelled the Great Dane's agitated scent and seen its tail pointing up in the air like a stick. He knew an attack was coming, and he was prepared for it. The only thing preventing him from acting was the fact that Yang Yan had subconsciously pulled tight on his leash. Despite this, Kelsang used his right shoulder to slam into his attacker. The Great Dane gained no advantage by attacking first.

Great Danes must have mastiff genes. When Genghis Khan defeated Europe, his army had with them a second army of Tibetan mastiffs. And so it was that the Mongols brought these fine dogs to Europe. Of course, this Great Dane couldn't know that the dog it faced had even purer blood flowing in his veins than it did.

Loosening the leash was a trick that the plump man used regularly. He made it look as if he was letting go by accident. The Doberman had had his ear torn, and the prize-winning German shepherd could never race again as a direct result of this underhanded trick. But the Great Dane's clumsy lurch forward was really only enough to make a smaller dog lose its balance and its chance to re-taliate. There was no greater skill to it than that. Kelsang, however, thought the Great Dane was about to attack his master, and with one firm tug he freed his chains from Yang Yan's hand.

The first clash. They were evenly matched, but the Great Dane was standing in a stronger position, and Kel-sang nearly lost his balance. Kelsang changed his tac-tics. His experience on the streets of Lhasa told him not to be too rash. When it came to size, he was no match for the Great Dane. In the second clash, the Great Dane trundled forward like a fully loaded truck, and Kelsang dodged it. Being so large, it couldn't change direction very quickly, and so Kelsang took the opportunity to sink his teeth into the other dog's shoulder. It ripped open like a piece of paper and seemed to detach from the rippling muscles underneath.

The Great Dane turned, howling in pain, and lunged at Kelsang again. Once more Kelsang took advantage of his nimbler frame and evaded the attack. But he wasn't going to give the Great Dane another chance, and he tore into its neck. Momentum propelled Kelsang forward, and he nearly lost his balance but recovered it just in time. His jaw muscles were powerful, and his teeth snapped the exposed vein in the other dog's neck.

The Great Dane seemed to want to keep fighting, but it could no longer support the weight of its own body. It fell, blood pouring from its wound. Kelsang kept his teeth firmly lodged in its neck. He had finally found a way to release the anger he felt over missing Han Ma. He shook his head but still didn't let go of the limp dog, all 175 pounds of it hanging from his mouth. Kelsang couldn't hear Yang Yan's shouting. Instead he narrowed his eyes and tried to imagine that he was reliving his triumphs against wolves up on the grasslands and the fights he had had against the dogs of Lhasa.

Finally, Kelsang threw the Great Dane's body to the ground. It was most definitely dead. He narrowed his red eyes under his dishevelled mess of fur and stared at the people who had gathered around. The plump man didn't dare make a sound. The hair on the back of Kelsang's neck flopped back down, and dragging his clanking chains with him, he made off in the direction of Yang Yan's house.

Yang Yan called after him, but Kelsang ignored his master. It took a scream loud enough to shatter glass to make Kelsang turn around and stare coldly at him, the hair on his neck standing on end again. Yang Yan swallowed what remained of his shout.

The crowd burst into laughter, despite having witnessed such ferocity. The plump man seemed to draw comfort from the crowd's reaction, and without checking whether his dog was really dead, said to Yang Yan, "What are you going to do, Mister? That was a purebred Great Dane."

By the time Yang Yan returned home, completely flustered, Kelsang was already lying in front of his kennel with his eyes closed, as if nothing had happened. Yang Yan edged toward him, concerned that Kelsang might still be agitated by the fight, but his expression was unusually calm. He wasn't going to jump at Yang Yan's outstretched hand.

Kelsang had finally given vent to his anger, and yet he still couldn't feel any love for the man standing before him. Even as he had been launching himself at the Great Dane, he hadn't been sure if he was doing it to protect Yang Yan or just to let out his frustration and hurt. Of course, protecting his master was an instinct that he couldn't be rid of, but he just couldn't love this man. He missed Han Ma more than ever. It was he who had cut him free from his collar. The thought made his neck tickle.

Yang Yan's voice was thick with hatred as he chained

Kelsang up again. "Nice one. I lost twenty thousand *yuan* because of you. But don't worry. I'll find a nice new home for you."

Kelsang ignored him, still deep in his own world. This irritated Yang Yan even more. The dog had paid no attention to his commands in front of all those people. He had been powerless. He didn't care about the money, but he couldn't stand such an arrogant, willful dog.

9

THE THREE GERMAN SHEPHERDS AT THE DEPARTMENT STORE

AS KELSANG WAS led into the yard behind the department store, he was greeted by three of the finest German shepherds he had ever seen. Their glossy brown coats and the chiseled outlines of their hind legs were the outcome of years of selective breeding and had won them prizes, but more important, they were great runners. They were purebreds. For the first time, Kelsang wasn't the superior dog, even though he was from the grasslands and had killed wolves.

The three German shepherds were locked up in a pen. After casting a glance at the intruder, they started barking in a way that only well-fed dogs can. Kelsang managed to take a look at them before being led into another pen.

The first was a powerful male whose long fur nearly

168

covered his eyes. He leapt at the wire mesh, barking furiously and revealing a row of somewhat damaged teeth in a mouth full of foaming spittle. No doubt he would try to shred Kelsang to pieces if he was let free. Kelsang was surprised to see how strong he was. He was even bigger than the biggest wolf he had ever seen. This was Zorro. The other smaller, rather immature male was Kaisa. He struggled to control his excitement, twirling like a spinning top after every few barks. The almost coal-black female, Susu, wasn't exactly barking but was attempting to chime in an accompaniment. She was fascinated by the silent Tibetan mastiff.

Kelsang saw that Zorro was the only worthy opponent among them. He had been honing this skill. Every time he arrived in a new place he would quickly assess who were his potential enemies.

That evening, when the security guards came to feed the three German shepherds, they made the fundamental error of opening both pens at the same time. They went to Kelsang's pen first, and he stepped out, curious to get to know the strange yard. But a few moments later, they opened the other pen, and without any warning, Zorro ran out and charged at Kelsang.

Kelsang was prepared, however. He may not have been expecting it at that very moment, but he had realized that it was going to happen sooner or later. He was ready, and fearless.

The fight turned out to be surprisingly simple. As Zorro leapt at him, baring his teeth, Kelsang darted to one side. He was in no hurry. In fact, he wanted to get a better sense of his opponent's strength. Zorro slid past, so Kelsang bit at his unprotected back, but Zorro was sensitive and turned half around to block Kelsang's sharp teeth with his head. All Kelsang could do was bite his shabby ear.

Once more they engaged in battle.

The two security guards stood aside, watching and shouting, the dog food sprinkled all around them on the ground. When the dogs broke apart again, the two men crept between them, their electric batons held high. The ends of the batons crackled and spat sparks, and a stench worse than burnt skin wafted toward Kelsang's nose. He had no plans to attack again. He had already sussed out Zorro's strength. And even though it was the first time he had seen an electric baton, he had a pretty good idea of its strength, too. It gave off the smell of something that had been set alight. The fact that man could create fire on the end of a stick was proof enough for him. There was no way he could fight such a weapon.

But Zorro was fuming at having his status challenged in this unprecedented manner. As he prepared to launch himself at Kelsang again, one of the electric batons came down on his neck. Letting out a howl of pain that seemed to rise from deep within him, his ferocity melted away, and he went scuttling back to his pen.

Kelsang was happy with his choice. The guards' weapons were extremely powerful, and while they might not be able to kill in an instant like a gun, they seemed to be able to sap an animal of its strength. That was all he needed to know.

Kelsang was kept alone in his pen. Every evening he watched as the three German shepherds were led toward the door of the huge building on the other side of the yard. In actual fact, it would be better to say that the dogs led the guards, so excited were they to get in. Kelsang couldn't figure out what could be so exciting.

A week later, there was another major theft at the department store, and Kelsang was chosen to replace the three German shepherds. Why should Kelsang take over from three superbly trained guard dogs? The reason was simple. He had received no training, and this was a major advantage.

The evening the man entered the store, he had been set upon by the three enormous German shepherds. They were too well trained to bark. As they sped toward him and prepared to leap, he held up his right hand. He was wearing a police uniform, and his command, one used in all police dog competitions, was clear and calm —"Stay!" It was just as he hoped. They could be easily controlled.

A police uniform, a flawless command and a perfect hand gesture. German shepherds trained by the police are very familiar with these things. They are branded in their memories through hours of training. Dogs that have retired from service cherish the memories of their days in the force. They are still working dogs and always will be.

The man's actions opened a connection in the dogs' brains to this part of their memory. Suddenly they were back with the policemen, part of the action. They stood still, and then as if under the spell of his hand, crouched down. They knew they had to do it quickly and expertly in order to receive praise from their master, which was probably only going to be an encouraging pat on the neck. But to a police dog, this was an incomparable honor.

The moment a police dog starts its training, it learns one principle that it never forgets — your master's command is everything. This becomes a conditioned reflex. And so it was that the three dogs came to obey this man so willingly. He was giving commands in a way that they hadn't experienced for a long time. It all came back to them so naturally. The three dogs lay there, not a hair out of place, their heart-shaped ears sticking up like shoots of bamboo, their eyes glistening. This is the first posture any police dog learns to perfect. Waiting, being prepared for the next move.

With everything under control, the man smiled at the dogs as they waited eagerly for praise. He wasn't going to disappoint them. He went to each in turn and patted them on the neck, receiving three grateful whimpers in return. Of course, he wasn't really there for the three docile dogs. His real goal was the watch counter.

The dogs remained loyal to his command as he broke open the lock. Dogs are only able to serve humans according to their instincts, and comprehensive training teaches them to do what they believe is correct without questioning it. They don't spend time thinking about whether what they are doing is logical or not. They are already convinced that the command itself doesn't matter. As long as it is given in the right way, it is always right to obey it.

Two hours later, a drowsy security guard made his rounds. To his surprise, he found the three dogs crouching beside the watch counter, as still as statues. Only then did he notice that the lock had been forced open and that all the most expensive watches were missing.

"My God!" the guard shouted. But still the dogs didn't react.

The first thought that came to the guard's mind was that he'd surely lose his job. Only after that did he realize that he should tell the dogs to move. They responded like well-oiled machines, staggering slightly after crouching in the same position for so long. They lined up beside him waiting for instructions.

"What a mess! A mess, a mess! The thief stole the stuff right under their noses!"

Without further ado, the dogs were stripped of their duties, locked in their pen and replaced by Kelsang. The guards led him into the department store through the back door. The interior was huge, and to Kelsang, who had been locked up in a small pen for over a week, it felt as big as a sports stadium. Suddenly he understood why the German shepherds had been so excited every evening.

After they untied his leash, Kelsang sensed that the
guards were watching him with suspicion. He trotted off
to inspect the four-story store. The floors were spotless,
the counters shiny clean, as if straight from a dream.
The only thing that made him uncomfortable was that
his breathing felt strange. He was still getting used to air-
conditioning.

In the food section on the ground floor, Kelsang spotted a caged pheasant, which made him very excited. The
bird shook with fear, leaping up and trying to fly around
its small cage, scattering feathers all over as the giant
dog approached.

Kelsang edged closer.

"Don't touch it!" The guard had been following him
the whole time.

Kelsang turned to look at him, and the sparkle in
his eyes vanished. He lay down beside a large, refresh-
ing refrigerated section. It reminded him of the Tibetan
grasslands. He ignored the men in uniforms gathering
around him.

"He's pretty lazy. He doesn't seem to want to move."

"In that case, he's no use to us. Purebred German
shepherds couldn't do the job, and now it looks like he
can't, either. But he is kind of cruel looking. Maybe that'll
be enough to scare the thieves away."

"Didn't the boss say the only reason the thief got
the better of those dogs was because they were so well
trained? That's why he brought us this one. No, wait. He
kept stressing that it was a mastiff. It won't follow any

old stranger's command. It's a guard dog. It doesn't need training to attack intruders."

The guards looked at Kelsang and felt their throats growing tight. They each went to a different part of the store to do their inspections.

Life had taken an unusually tranquil turn for Kelsang. Every evening, after the sun went down and he had been fed, a guard would lead him into the store and undo his chains. He was then free to do as he pleased. Within the first few days, he had familiarized himself with every corner of the store, and now, most evenings, he made straight for the refrigerated counters where he lay down to sleep. The cool air was comforting.

With Kelsang on guard, nothing went missing in the store. The security guards were still unsure whether this detached, unapproachable dog was really qualified for the job, but as long as nothing disappeared, that was the most important thing.

Kelsang barely saw the other three dogs now as he spent most of his days curled up asleep in his pen. He knew that Zorro was watching his every move, but he didn't want to get into a fight. This wasn't the time. Besides, the guards weren't going to let it happen. Every morning, as he was led back into his pen, and every evening, as he was led out to the store, his chains were on.

But eventually, opportunities always present themselves.

One morning, as Kelsang was being led from the back door of the store into the compound, something distracted the guard, and he merely slipped Kelsang's chains over the open gate of his pen before running off.

Kelsang never would have guessed that the day of reckoning would come so soon. He watched coldly as Zorro, who was in the yard, stalked toward him. Then he shook his head so that the chains fell to the ground, no longer restricting his movements.

The chains were still heavy around his neck, but they didn't slow him in any way. After the year of being tied up on the mountainside by the man with the dark cheeks, he had grown accustomed to them and had built up strong neck muscles.

After a few brief rounds, Zorro realized that he was just being played with. No matter how much he pounced and bit, he couldn't hurt the burly black dog. He became angrier with each attack, not once able to get the upper hand.

Kelsang was like a ghost. Each time he slipped out of Zorro's reach, he would manage to twist around and tug playfully on a clump of his fur.

The first time Kelsang fought with Zorro, he hadn't been sure how to fight a dog of his own caliber. He paused and faltered. Yet he now realized that if he wanted to, he could finish off Zorro without any problems.

Maybe it was because he found his store job so depressing, or more likely, he was just realizing, it was because he wanted to show off in front of Susu, but he was in no hurry to put Zorro out of his misery. So confident that he could win whenever he wanted, he chased the panting German shepherd around in circles.

Once Zorro realized that he was a mouse being chased by a cat, all he wanted was for it to end. Despite his furious barking and continuous leaping, he was clearly getting weaker. He was going mad. There was no way he could grab hold of this shadow of a dog flitting in front of him.

Kelsang, meanwhile, was more concerned with making his movements elegant and beautiful to look at, because even though he hadn't looked around to check, he knew that Susu's gaze was fixed on him.

Finally, an exhausted Zorro made one last push, lost his balance and fell to the ground. Kelsang seemed to float down on top of him, his chains trailing behind. He placed one paw on Zorro's chest, and in a flash as quick as lightning, sank his teeth into the exhausted dog.

If one of the guards hadn't rushed over just in time, Zorro would probably have died out there on the concrete yard. The man's shouts brought Kelsang to his senses, and he held back, just nicking the skin on Zorro's neck.

"Mr. Yang was right. He can't be left with the other dogs. There's no dog that could beat him," the guard said.

"I only left him for a minute! At least it looks like he showed Zorro some mercy."

"Sometimes he won't let me close when I'm feeding him, but still he's not like the other dogs — always barking. He just narrows his eyes and growls. It's terrifying. Step back."

"Don't you have your baton?"

"Are you brave enough to use a baton on him? I'm not."

"Me, neither," the other guard admitted.

Kelsang had already slunk back into his pen, dragging his chains behind him. Their clanking reminded him of his life out in the open with Han Ma.

And so it was that without much effort, Kelsang became the leader. Not that he cared much. More important to him was that he now had his sights set on Susu, the beautiful inky black German shepherd, even if he could only catch a glimpse of her as he went out to the store in the evening or when he came back early in the morning. Once back in his pen, all he did was sleep.

The day finally arrived.

Even though he hadn't exactly been waiting for it, Kelsang knew that he wasn't being let loose in the store for his own pleasure. The security guards hadn't tried to teach him anything, but he still understood that the store was supposed to be empty. It was his job to make sure it stayed that way.

At first light, Kelsang heard a noise. He was lying beside one of the refrigeration units, enjoying the cold air and reminiscing about his first experience of snow up on the grasslands. Until now, not even the hum of the motor had shaken him from his daydream.

The noise was coming from the jewelry department on the second floor. Kelsang didn't like it up there. The lights always made him feel dizzy. Nevertheless, he decided to check it out.

He walked up the stairs, paused at the top and looked around. Everything was quiet. He took a few steps forward, and still there was no sound. It had probably been a mouse. The mice in the store were particularly fat and sluggish, with a remarkable tenacity and bravery to boot. They were always crashing around and knocking things over. Still, they always managed to escape before Kelsang could get close. They were small enough to hide comfortably in cracks that he couldn't even push his nose into. In any case, he wasn't bored enough to bother chasing them.

Yet something was making Kelsang uneasy. The mice usually only appeared in the food section downstairs. They had never been up here before. He threaded his way between the counters that were lit up like shining islands bathed in summer sunlight. The lights were specially designed to make the jewelry look dazzling and beautiful.

He found nothing. It must have been a mouse.

Kelsang looked up one last time before making his way back downstairs. He sniffed at the cool air. Suddenly he detected a strange smell. It was probably just a bag of candy one of the store clerks had stashed in a cupboard, or someone's perfume. But the customers had long since gone, and these scents should have grown faint by now.

But the strange smell kept wafting into Kelsang's nostrils, and it was getting stronger. It was no different than other smells, coming suddenly and disappearing just as quickly, but it didn't smell like anything he'd experienced before. Or was it like mud after the rain?

Smell was an important tool for Kelsang's imagination. He could smell that someone had been lingering in front of the counter. Whoever it was must have climbed in through the window, since he could detect traces of the scent in the dust on the window frame. It was a smoker. The person behind the smell became clearer, like a road opening out before him. Growing more and more excited, Kelsang jogged in pursuit of the smell. He knew he was close.

The smell was getting stronger. He could detect a hint of fear, a smell people normally didn't give off. Fear has its own particular smell, and Kelsang understood it well.

One day the previous week, he had been led into the store and tied to a post near the door. The security guards hadn't got around to untying him before he found someone hiding near the restroom. The man shouted as he was led away. The smells of the day's customers were still fresh, but it was the smell of fear that told him the man was there. It couldn't be washed off like other smells.

Once again, Kelsang knew that this person wasn't supposed to be here. The only people allowed in the store at night wore black uniforms. He knew their smell, and this person definitely didn't smell like one of them. The smell was coming from behind some potted plants beside the escalators. Kelsang couldn't see anything, but his nose was sure. Someone was hiding back there.

There was a row of plastic chairs against the wall behind the plants where customers could rest. If Kelsang were to squeeze behind the chairs, he would have no room to turn around and get out. So he did what he always used to do when faced with wolves in hiding about to pounce on his flock of sheep. He retreated a few steps and then started barking. He then ran around the potted plants barking even more. The wolves always emerged, fearing that his master would soon arrive.

The intruder was no more patient or intelligent than the wolves, and so out he came. But nor was he as quick and elegant. He stumbled out, his trousers catching on the branches of a potted plant. He stopped.

He raised his right hand and calmly gave his command. Only then did he realize that the dog in front of him wasn't a German shepherd but a breed he had never seen before. Furthermore, it was looking at him with unmistakable contempt. There was clearly no point in giving it any instructions, and he suddenly felt ridiculous.

He pulled out his knife, but by the time he realized how stupid this was, it was too late. Somehow he had believed that this dog could be silenced as the German shepherds had been, that it was just a matter of finding the right command. But he had miscalculated.

A sting at his waist. The knife dropped to the ground and spun out of sight. He also lost a sleeve.

Without giving him any time to prepare, Kelsang went for the man's throat. The man crossed his hands over his face, and the other sleeve was gone.

By the time the security guards made it to the second floor, they were faced with a peculiar scene. An almost naked man was lying on top of a large, shaky screen, and Kelsang was sitting facing him, howling furiously.

"Please, save me!" the man sobbed. "What took you so long? It nearly ate me. Where did you get this dog? I'm making a complaint!"

No matter how hard they tried to persuade him, the man wouldn't move. Only when the guard who usually fed Kelsang crept up and fastened the chains to his collar did the man climb down, sobbing gratefully.

Kelsang was still livid and ready to charge at him. It took two security guards to hold him back.

From that day until Kelsang left the store six months later, there were no more incidents of burglary. Of course, that didn't include shoplifters who made off with small items during the day. But word spread among the more serious thieves in the area that a terrifying dog, straight from the grasslands, was guarding the store.

10

SUSU IS GONE

KELSANG'S LIFE AT the department store was peaceful and comfortable. He was fed special dog food every day, and he could almost feel himself growing and maturing as he slept in his pen. His work required no physical strain, and he was used to it. All he had to do after the store closed at the end of the day was patrol in search of anyone who had hidden in a corner or snuck in.

Kelsang's help made life much easier for the security guards. They didn't even need to make their hourly rounds. All they had to do was release him inside in the evening and lead him back out in the morning. The night was theirs to do as they pleased — watch movies, sleep, play computer games. Somehow they didn't realize the potential downside of the situation. If only one person was needed to collect Kelsang, there was no need to employ so many security guards. But being totally unaware of this, they spent their nights in the computer section playing the latest release. That night it was the newest installment of *Devil Beast*.

And so it was that Kelsang was left to roam the large store. The many smells of the day were being dispersed by the air-conditioning, and yet Kelsang went in search of new ones that lingered on. He was already perfectly familiar with his responsibilities as guard dog. The store was his terrain, and the only people allowed in were the security guards. It wasn't difficult for Kelsang to adjust to this life. The store was just a new pasture for him, and he applied the same principles he had used when protecting the sheep and his master's yurt. Intruders were to be met with a full-on attack. Only this time, he was protecting aisle after aisle of food and miscellaneous goods.

It wasn't such a big leap to go from imagining the store as his grasslands to seeing the vibrant green spread out before him. Suddenly everything felt familiar. Open spaces had always awakened Kelsang's desire to run, and he needed exercise to vent his untamed nature. He gathered speed, rounding the aisles without slowing down, sliding across the shiny floors like a car on a race track. Then he made for the next large room.

Life was simpler here than on the grasslands — no rushing around after lost sheep, no getting up in the middle of the night to check around the yurt. Kelsang was driven to run by instinct. But somehow he believed that one day he'd make it back to the grasslands and be a shepherd dog again.

With plenty of nutrition, rest and exercise, Kelsang was in the best possible shape, mentally and physically.

Not one pound of food went to waste. His muscles were as hard as rock. At over 175 pounds, he was like a bear running down the aisles. His glossy mane fluttered as he ran, like threads of silk in a summer breeze. Until now he wouldn't have been anyone's first choice to star in a shampoo commercial, but things were changing.

Spring in the north finally arrived. Every day, as Kelsang awoke in his pen, the fragrance of mud and grass wafted toward him on the wind.

He began to be roused by an indescribable emotion. He didn't know what it was. He had experienced spring up on the grasslands — the small flowers nestled close to the ground, waiting for the snow to melt so that they could bloom. The flowers always used to surprise him when he was a small pup. The pollen made him sneeze, and Tenzin's family would burst into peals of laughter — a rare sound in that camp — as he scratched his nose with his paw. From then on he hated all flowers, and spring made him anxious.

But this was a completely different feeling. All Kelsang's waking moments were occupied with despondent thoughts, and sometimes he even forgot his desire to see Han Ma, he was so consumed by them. Before, he would wake up furious at his betrayal and instantly start pawing at the metal mesh fence of his pen and jumping and running around. But this new feeling seemed to be taking control of him. He didn't understand what was happening.

The only relief he could find was to circle the pen, pressing his body tight against the mesh, just like a panther locked up at the zoo. All he wanted was to keep walking. He had no particular destination in mind. Maybe he could walk toward the horizon? But he was in the city and couldn't even see the horizon.

That evening, as the sun was setting, Kelsang suddenly found his destination. It was a noise that first alerted him. He looked up and saw Susu standing in the other pen, watching him through the mesh. He wanted to get closer to her. That was all he could think about. So that was it, he realized. He wanted to be beside Susu.

Ever since he'd been beaten, Zorro seemed to abandon his once provocative behavior. Kelsang was receiving special treatment. He ate and patrolled on his own now. He had stopped paying attention to the other dogs long ago, and although he sometimes heard Zorro barking, all it took was one look, and the German shepherd would fall silent again.

This is how it works in the dog world — power decides everything. A pack's leader is always the strongest and smartest.

Today it was as if Kelsang was seeing Susu for the first time. Beautiful, black Susu. He thought back to that first day he had arrived at the department store. There had been a pair of black eyes watching him. But he couldn't shake off the feeling that German shepherds were his natural-born enemies. This was what experience told him, at least — the snippets he had gathered since leaving the grasslands, wandering the streets of Lhasa and being tied up on that mountainside. Experience was what he believed in most.

But something in his heart was telling him to renounce it. As soon as the security guard fastened the chains to his collar and opened the pen, Kelsang dragged him in the direction of the German shepherds. The guards had never tried to prevent Kelsang from doing anything before, but then he had never had any special demands. In any case, there was no way one person could stop Kelsang from going where he wanted.

This was Kelsang's second big emotional adventure. The first had started when Han Ma stroked his fur. Kelsang hesitated, unsure if he was doing the right thing. His previous experience couldn't help him now.

Zorro's teeth glinted in the corner of the pen, but he didn't move. Kaisa, in contrast, looked up in excitement and wagged his tail furiously.

Susu pressed her nose up to the mesh. Kelsang detected a new smell that somehow reminded him of his mother's, now a distant memory. But it wasn't quite the same. He flared his nostrils and went closer. He needed more of it.

When Kelsang and Susu touched noses, a shock shot through him, and he turned around to look at the guard. This was the first time since leaving the grasslands that he had looked to a human to tell him what to do. The guard was indifferent. The all-night gaming sessions were starting to take their toll.

The second time Kelsang's nose brushed against Susu's, a tremble went from the tip of his nose down through every hair on his body, blocking out the sound of Zorro's desperate barking and Kaisa's flat accompaniment.

After the guard took Kelsang into the store and undid his chains, Kelsang stood still for a long time. Eventually, he turned and sniffed at the breeze coming through the crack under the door that had been closed behind him. He wanted to see if he could smell Susu.

One of the other security guards noticed. "He seems different today. You don't think he's found something, do you?"

"No, but he might have fallen in love with Susu. What kind of dog would you get if you crossed a German shepherd with a Tibetan mastiff?"

The two guards continued joking as they made their way up to the computer department, leaving Kelsang where he was. That night he didn't do any running but went to the refrigerated section and dozed in the cool air.

From that day on, it became a sort of ritual. Every day, before and after work, Kelsang would approach Susu's pen without really understanding what he was doing. But of one thing he was sure. He only felt contented once he had touched noses with Susu. He didn't know what was going to happen next. No one had taught him about the birds and the bees up on the grasslands, and he had been alone ever since then. Of course, Zorro was not happy about this, but all he could do was hide in his corner and growl helplessly.

Had everything continued, no doubt Kelsang would have become an excellent guard dog, and he and Susu could have brought many puppies into the world, and they in turn would have been excellent guard dogs. The natural strength of their mastiff father would have been honed by the discipline and training of their German shepherd mother. They could even have created a new breed that would have become the police dog of choice. But anyone can spend their time imagining things that are never destined to come to pass.

That evening, as the sun was setting, and after Kelsang had finished his nose-touching ritual with Susu, the guards rushed him into the store. They tugged off his chains, keen to get to their computer game. Kelsang turned for his routine sniff at the crack under the door when a smell hit him like a bolt of lightning. It was one that he recognized dimly, but because he hadn't smelled it in so long, it felt half unknown.

As if in a trance, he followed the smell up to the third floor where the small handicraft stalls could be found. The store rented out space to individual traders to get more customers through the doors. Kelsang located the source of the smell — a small cabinet that had been empty until yesterday. He slowed. He knew this smell. It was as if it came from his own body. He had grown up in this smell. It came from the grasslands.

The stall had just been rented by a Tibetan trader who had brought with her small trinkets from the plateau. Kelsang didn't want to leave the cabinet with its wooden bowls the color of amber, the jewelry that had once decorated Mistress's neck and waist, the knives that Tenzin used to carry with him, the boxes made from yak bone. Kelsang was in a dream. He was back on the grasslands and could smell the smoke rising from the yurt.

When he emerged from the store the next morning, he didn't go to Susu's pen but made straight for his own, lay down and began to think. He was replaying his life on the grasslands and all that had happened to him since leaving. It was only when one of the guards came around midday to give him food that Kelsang discovered that Susu had vanished. Zorro and Kaisa were the only ones left in the pen.

The guard was pouring out his food when he felt Kelsang's chains leap up as if they'd been bitten by a poisonous snake. This was followed by a muffled thunder, which echoed around the yard, as the chains were pulled across the concrete.

A vision of the enemy appeared before Kelsang's eyes, a figure traced from the unfamiliar smell lingering in the air. He had taken Susu away. It was him.

Kelsang dragged his chains toward the other pen and started banging his weight against the reinforced gate. No one was strong enough to control him, and the guards could only watch as the huge dog thrashed against the pen. The two remaining German shepherds started to bark, but something made them stop and they retreated to a corner, whimpering.

If Kelsang's wild nature had softened since leaving the grasslands, his recent good mood — a survival tactic he had been developing here at the store — was now gone forever. He was a mastiff, and he was wild with fury at having lost his companion.

Eventually, Kelsang managed to burst open the gate to the pen. The two dogs wailed as if their day of reckoning had arrived, but Kelsang suddenly became very calm. He turned and went to lie down in the middle of the yard. Susu's scent felt very far away. Zorro and Kaisa weren't going to wait for another opportunity like this and escaped from the pen.

After the bell sounded to announce the store closing for the day, the security guards had no choice but to pluck up their courage and enter the yard. The look on Kelsang's face suggested that his good-natured cooperation was over.

He watched as they crept closer. There was something about their careful movements, or perhaps it was just the chains they were carrying, that suddenly made Kelsang come to his senses. He roared, telling them to keep their distance, and the men understood.

Eventually, however, one young man started to approach Kelsang. He often bragged about kicking an army dog to death when he'd trained as a special agent. He was like a cocksure cowboy approaching an untamed foal, but it was obviously pointless. There was a line that Kelsang wasn't going to let him cross without a fight.

In truth, this young man had probably only ever worked in army kitchens. He stumbled back, flushed, with no shirt and two red scratches down his chest.

The security guards had no choice but to replace Kelsang with the two German shepherds. Delighted, and with renewed self-confidence at having his job back, Zorro started barking as soon as his leash was attached. He charged at Kelsang, who was sitting casually on top of the two halves of the young man's uniform. It reminded Zorro of his days in the police force when all the dogs used to wait to have their leashes fastened before being led outside.

No one understood what happened next. By the time Kelsang had settled back down on the ripped uniform, Zorro was lying in a pool of fresh blood, his leg twitching but his amber eyes already lifeless. Zorro was just another, albeit more solid, uniform to be discarded on the ground. Kaisa tore away from his leash. He scuttled back to the pen, his tail between his legs, and buried himself in the far corner.

When Yang Yan came the next day to collect Kelsang, the dog didn't attack him as the security guards expected he would. Indeed, the mastiff put up no resistance at all and was easily led into the boss's car. The guards had refused to have him back in the store. It was as simple as that.

No one knew where Susu had gone, although the

guards must have had some idea because the gate to the pen was always locked. The deal was probably done in the afternoon. No one would have seen the truck pull into the yard, nor would they have seen Susu climb into it, trembling but still obeying orders.

Somebody must have seen her at some point, though, probably on a plate in a restaurant. So you should always watch out for what is going in and out of trucks.

The next day, Kelsang was loaded into a cage, and again he made no resistance. He was being taken to the botanical gardens on the outskirts of the city.

"There's no other way. I tried to contact you at the time, honest. I phoned before I took him to the store, but you didn't answer. Your boss told me you'd gone south for a meeting. No one can control him. Just as long as someone can take him — anyone — a circus, a zoo, a fire station, whatever. You know how much I lost when he killed that Great Dane? He was a great help at the store, though."

"It wasn't a meeting. I was delivering a special machine to one of the kids who has difficulty walking."

"And it took that long?"

"He needed to learn how to use it."

"What was it, a machine from outer space? How long could it take for a kid to learn to use a walking stick?"

"It wasn't just the machine. He had to do physical therapy, too."

"Well, all I've done is taken the dog to the botanical

gardens. They're doing me a favor by looking after him."

"Have you forgotten? If it wasn't for him, we'd never have survived that trip up from the plateau. You'd never have made it back to your fancy house with your garden and pool."

"I haven't done anything to him, I swear."

Of course, Kelsang never found out about the argument Yang Yan and Han Ma had over the phone. He was busy adjusting to his new surroundings, and in the week since he'd arrived, he had no complaints. He had wanted to get out of the store, and now he sensed that things were about to get even better. It was just a matter of waiting peacefully. He was no longer the young mastiff from the grasslands who only thought about fighting wolves and who gathered experience as he gathered scars. By now he was experienced enough. He had grown up.

His new iron cage was located in a cluster of lilac bushes and had originally been built to store garden equipment. Every day at sunset, an old man, who looked like a stone blown smooth by the wind, came with a bucket and flask. He would tighten Kelsang's chains — the same ones he had arrived in, as they had been informed that he was a mastiff from the grasslands and that it was best to keep their distance — before unlocking the door. He scrubbed the dog's food and water bowls, gave him his day's rations, swept the cage clean and then locked the door again. Only then did he loosen the chains.

"Okay, beautiful dog. It's getting dark, so eat up. I know you want to go for a run, but I can't let you out.

I don't have the strength to hold you, and I can't be re-
sponsible for you escaping. The boss says you're valu-
able, and I've got to take good care of you. Anyway, it
wouldn't be good if you scared the visitors, would it? But
we do want them to see you — you might bring more
of them in. What am I saying? Is this the botanical gardens or the zoo? But there's only one of you in the city,
and you must be lonely, just like me. Whatever you do,
don't be like me." As the old man rambled on, his hands
moved continuously, cleaning the cage of the garbage
thrown in by visitors.

In fact, not many people bothered Kelsang during
the day, and he could spend much of it lying in his cage,
sleeping under the dense shade of the lilacs. Most people came to see the exotic imported plants, such as the
sea coconut seedlings being nursed in the greenhouse.
Whenever anyone did venture into the lilac thicket, they
paid no attention to him, at most thinking that he was
an unusual animal before walking on.

But that day a child lingered in front of Kelsang's cage,
an ice cream dribbling down his hand. He was calling
out some strange name, something soft and cute sounding that would never be heard in the rough environment
of the grasslands. It was far more suited to a small, cud-
dly pet dog than to a mastiff.

"Fluffy, are you sleeping? Do you want some ice
cream?" the little boy called in his soft voice as he pushed
his hand through the bars.

Kelsang didn't look up at first but cast a glance at the

child out of the corner of his eye. He clearly wasn't planning on leaving any time soon. He reminded Kelsang of Tenzin's son. Both of them smelled as though they'd been doused from head to toe in milk. Their voices sounded similar, too, even though they'd grown up thousands of miles apart. He slowly looked up at the child.

"Come on, Fluffy. It's hot. Why don't you have some?" The boy was now waving his dribbling ice cream at Kelsang.

Kelsang licked the ice cream very carefully. This was the first time a child had approached him since he'd left the grasslands. He twisted his tongue around the dessert slowly, as if worried that he might scare the boy. It was eerie how much he looked like Tenzin's son. Once the ice cream was gone, Kelsang started licking the boy's hand, stopping only when he started giggling from the tickles.

A shout came from beyond the lilacs, and Kelsang watched as the little boy disappeared. He continued sniffing at the bars where his smell lingered. It would soon be completely smothered by the scent of lilacs.

This was the only thing about the gardens that made Kelsang a little unhappy. The thick lilac fragrance often made him feel drowsy. Of all the smells he had encountered, this one was the most powerful. It swept over everything like a wave, surging up high and falling back down again, with Kelsang a delicate sampan riding on its crest. He was a sea swallow soaring above the waves of the perfume.

When the old man came that evening, he discovered yesterday's food and water still in their bowls and Kelsang pacing around his cage. Every once in a while, he would stop and sniff in the direction of the main gate, where it smelled least of lilacs.

"Are you sick, doggie? But you look as strong as a little ox. Are you homesick? I don't know where your home is. All I know is the boss said a rich man brought you, so you must have had a nice life before. You're not used to such crude conditions, is that it? But don't you think it's lovely here?"

The old man's monologue was interrupted by a sharp clang from the cage. To his surprise, Kelsang jumped up on his hind legs, his front paws pressed against the bars, his eyes fixed in the direction of the main gate. Kelsang's nostrils were flapping open and closed as he attempted to breathe in more air. It was a smell, a beautiful smell, and he wanted more of it.

Han Ma.

It was the merest hint of him at first, and it came and went. He was still far away, but Kelsang knew he was coming. He started trembling ever so slightly in anticipation.

"What happened?" the old man asked, resting on his broom and looking down the path worn through the lilacs by impatient visitors.

No one, no bird call, nothing. The gardens were closing, and everyone had already left.

What was happening?

Half a minute later, Han Ma appeared, hurrying toward Kelsang.

Unable to wait any longer, Kelsang barked, ramming his body against the side of his cage, making its sturdy iron bars shake.

"Are you his owner?" the old man asked Han Ma. "I've been feeding him for a week, and he hasn't made a peep. He's been waiting like that for ages. He must have been able to smell you."

"I'm here now," said Han Ma, walking up to the cage and reaching inside.

Kelsang had been waiting for him for so long. Trembling with happiness, he closed his eyes and pressed his head into Han Ma's hands, the hands that had cut the metal collar from his neck.

After a while, the old man interrupted the reunion, eager to open the cage and let the dog out to meet his owner properly. Kelsang didn't make a big scene — wagging his tail and yapping like other dogs would have. He was from the grasslands, and he wasn't good at that sort of thing. He did feel the need to show his emotions, but he just didn't know how. On the grasslands, he had always lived according to some notion of duty, but what he felt for Han Ma was a magnificent emotion that came from deep within him. Love — that was what he felt for Han Ma — a deep love.

Han Ma stroked Kelsang's large head. The dog didn't make any noise but just pressed closer to his master's leg. Han Ma could feel him trembling.

Yang Yan arrived with the manager of the gardens just in time to see man and dog reunited.

"I looked after him for so long, and he never let me touch his head," Yang Yan muttered to himself jealously.

"From now on, I'll look after you," said Han Ma, picking purple lilac blossoms from Kelsang's coat. "You're my dog, and I won't let anyone put you in a cage ever again."

11

GUIDE DOG

THEIR TEACHER, HAN MA, said he was bringing them a pet, but the students at the School for Deaf and Blind Children didn't realize just how big that pet would be. It took Han Ma a long time to persuade the principal that Kelsang was indeed a dog, not a bear from a disbanded circus. The school had never had a pet before, and the principal only agreed that the dog could stay on the condition that his chains were never removed.

When Kelsang entered the classroom for the first time, a crowd of young children, their eyes round and dark, surrounded him. He felt scared and withdrew, unwilling to take another step forward. The bright lights and shiny floors also made him feel uncomfortable.

Suddenly one of the girls screamed, perhaps out of excitement or because another child had pushed her. The hair on the back of Kelsang's neck stood on end, and he roared in reply.

The children froze in fear.

Han Ma stroked Kelsang gently while scolding him

and then continued to lead him into the center of the room. The number of children swelled, but Kelsang sensed that Han Ma was not afraid of them. In fact, he had a sort of authority over them. He trusted Han Ma, and as long as his master wasn't scared, he wouldn't be, either. These children were not like the ones Kelsang had met before, and it wasn't just because they wore dark glasses. It was the way they twisted their bodies in search of Han Ma's voice, and they all had such lively faces.

The first child reached out cautiously to touch him, but Kelsang stiffened, unable to control his reaction. This was a stranger's hand, after all. Han Ma gently stroked his back. Gradually, as each hand felt its way toward him, Kelsang discovered that they weren't as rough as he was expecting. They landed gently on his back, as soft as feathers. They had no intention of hurting him. In fact, they were warming, like the setting sun high up on the plateau. Kelsang relaxed. One little girl stroked his bristly moustache, but when he stuck out his tongue to lick her hand, she withdrew like a startled animal.

"Don't worry. He's just licking you," Han Ma reassured her as she stroked the hand that had been "attacked" by Kelsang's tongue. Slowly, she reached out again. Her hand was one of the few tools at her disposal for understanding the world around her. Kelsang licked it once more, and she cried out in delight and began giggling.

At that moment, the principal happened to pass by. He had been trying to come up with an excuse to get rid of this animal — was it really a dog? — but the sight of the little girl made the thought vanish in a puff of smoke. This child had been abandoned in a trash can at the train station when she was a baby. She was now five years old, and he had never seen her laugh before. One after another, the children reached out to let Kelsang lick their hands. Each lick was met with helpless laughter. The principal had never heard these children laugh like this — they were usually so taciturn. He slipped away without saying a word.

Kelsang didn't really like children. He had never taken much interest in mini humans. But these little ones with their dark glasses were like extra special, gentle sheep. Their hands rested so softly on his coat, like easily startled birds fluttering down to earth to find food. The children belonged to Han Ma, and he would do anything for his master. Of that he was sure.

When Han Ma first came to the school, he told the children all about birds. Holding one in his hands, he showed them its feathers, its small claws and the wings it used to fly. When he opened his hands the bird flew away, leaving only the sound of its wings beating in the air.

In a similar way, Kelsang became the very definition of a dog for the blind children. Dogs were large, with warm tongues, long fur that was especially thick around the neck, ears that flopped on either side of their heads, and curly tails. Han Ma had never thought of Kelsang as an unusual dog, but when some of the children regained their sight as adults, their subsequent encounters with our canine friends resulted in a certain disappointment. Was it just that time had made their memory of the dog back at the school sweeter and more perfect? They must have lifted up their hands, the hands that they had used instead of eyes, and asked themselves, could they have fooled me?

One day a journalist came to the school to write a story. On his way out, he saw something truly incredible — a huge dog walking with firm, steady steps, with one young child holding its collar and two more children holding hands walking behind them. The dog waited patiently for them to catch up, and when necessary, it would stop, turn and grunt.

"What's going on?" The journalist wasn't sure what he was seeing.

"Nothing. He's just taking the children to the canteen."

"My God, I've never seen such a large guide dog!" the journalist said, sounding almost hysterical, and he took a photo that appeared in the newspaper the next day.

The children at the school were already used to Kelsang. He had learned to lead them across the playground to the canteen and even out to a nearby shop so that they could buy things. If ever any of the children fell over or had any problems as they were moving about, Kelsang would be the first to help. Within moments, the echo of his heavy paws could be heard in the courtyard, and he would be by their side. He could detect what smell had brought the children there and was ready to take them wherever they wanted to go. He could distinguish between the shop, the canteen, the classroom and the dormitories, and was able to take them to their beds without the slightest hiccup.

Kelsang was happy that he could develop his shepherding skills in this way. These little sheep really needed him, and they were Han Ma's most precious property. He looked after them as best he could, took them outside to enjoy the sun and even acted as a soft rug for them to play on.

But the nights belonged to Kelsang alone. In the stillness, when everyone was sleeping, he would stir from his spot in front of Han Ma's door and loop around the courtyard. Then he would jump over the wall from one of the flowerbeds into the cornfield on the other side. He learned to run through the rows of corn without damaging a single leaf, like a ghost blown along by the wind. He sniffed greedily at the earth and the fresh green growth.

He had fallen back into his habit of running. When he ran, everything around him was a blur. It was like leaving all his troubles, his bad memories behind him.

One night, when the moon was full and the corn was ripening in the field, Kelsang spotted a farmer up ahead. He was leaning against a shack smoking. Kelsang didn't think to avoid him and swept past. Before the farmer could react, Kelsang had shot into the depths of the cornfield, leaving only the rustling of leaves whipped up by the air rushing behind him.

The farmer thought he was seeing things. Had a bear

just run past? He was from the Greater Khingan Mountains, in the northeastern corner of China, home to acres of dense forest and plump animals. In this mosquito-infested farmland far from home, that was what he wanted to believe. He was sure that a bear had come to steal his corn, but that it could smell the hunter in him — something that had been passed down for generations from father to son — and that was why it had run away.

But for some reason, the farmer's story didn't catch on. Kelsang only let himself be seen that one time, and even though the locals had read in their schoolbooks about bears stealing corn, the grinding routine of daily life had erased their ability to imagine it happening in their own fields. Of course, they hadn't heard that a bear had recently escaped from Harbin Zoo. They'd rather believe that the sewers of Paris were home to tens of thousands of crocodiles than that there was a bear roaming their cornfields.

In any case, Kelsang only ever let himself run freely like this at night. Before the sun came up, he always returned to the school, the morning dew like pearls in his coat. He would jump back over the wall into the courtyard, where he did a few more laps, and satisfied that all was as it should be, plopped down at Han Ma's door. Every morning, when Han Ma emerged for his run, Kelsang was there waiting for him.

Each day a large group from the school appeared on the main road, Kelsang trotting beside Han Ma and behind them a line of children. Kelsang was always happy when he was with Han Ma and would run beside him energetically. They would do a lap around the village, through the streets that smelled of grain, then go back to the school, where the children would gesture to Han Ma, "What a fine morning! The sun is so warm! What lovely fresh air!" Their world was so beautiful.

Kelsang was becoming a truly excellent guide dog. While he had not yet ventured onto busy streets with the blind children, his ample frame meant he could easily handle daily tasks such as taking them across the street nearby. But he was an exception. Most guide dogs are gentle and docile because people usually choose breeds that are obedient and non-aggressive by nature, such as collies, Labradors or golden retrievers. No one could have imagined that a mastiff with the wilds of Tibet coursing through his veins would make a good guide dog.

That August, Han Ma received a letter notifying him that he had been accepted into the Chinese Youth Volunteer Corps. He was to serve as a primary school teacher in Hulun Buir, Inner Mongolia. Not wanting to upset the children, he left one morning before anyone had woken up, taking Kelsang with him. But it was a painful morning nevertheless, and some say the children are still waiting for Han Ma to return and take them into the village.

12

KELSANG RETURNS TO THE GRASSLANDS

HULUN BUIR, ONE OF the world's four great swathes of pastureland.

Kelsang could already smell it through the car's dirty windows — the smell of lush grass. He was restless and kept twisting around to try to catch a glimpse out to see if he was right. Their driver recoiled in fright at the sight of the huge, jumpy dog in his rearview mirror, as Han Ma stroked Kelsang on the neck, trying to calm him.

Kelsang started scratching at the crack beneath the door and pressing his nose up to it with a greedy urgency, drawing the outside air deep into his lungs. It had been so long since he had inhaled such beautifully fresh air, but there was something unfamiliar about it, too. It wasn't exactly the same as the air up on the Tibetan plateau. Still, the smell of crushed grass was like a wall pressing against his chest. He bashed his head against the car door, growling in agitation.

"It's okay, be patient." Han Ma couldn't help but be affected by Kelsang's mood, so he asked the driver to stop the car. His dog had been cooped up for too long, he said, and needed to go outside and run around.

Kelsang stood on the slope looking out over a wide sweep of grassland. He stood there a long time without moving, save for the rise and fall of his rib cage. After a while, he started to shift his paws, cautiously at first because the grass was tickly. His heart was beating faster and faster, and the grass was rippling in the wind. He leaned down to sniff the lush, luxuriant pasture. The soil here was so much more fertile than up on the Tibetan plateau.

He felt drunk from the smell, and ignoring Han Ma's calls, began to run. There was no end to the grasslands. They undulated into the distance as far as the eye could see. He kept running, and when he turned to look back, the car was as small as a beetle, the tiniest dot on the horizon.

He was feeling much calmer by the time he made it back to Han Ma's side, yet before climbing back into the car, he stopped once more to gaze out on the verdant pasture rippling in the wind.

"Okay, you'll have plenty of time to look at the grass," Han Ma said, pulling Kelsang into the car.

The school was in a large enclosed campus on the outskirts of a small town, with two big brick buildings — one for the teachers' accommodations and offices, and the other containing the classrooms. The term had not yet started, so Han Ma and Kelsang had a couple of weeks of free time to settle in.

On the third day, Han Ma decided to head out into the grasslands with his camera. This was his first outing with Kelsang since arriving in Hulun Buir, and they set off at dawn. He had borrowed a horse, but only after its owner assured him that it had never thrown anyone.

Autumn on the grasslands is serene, with the livestock busy gobbling up as much food as they can before the arrival of the cruel winter. They have to accumulate enough fat so that they will have a fighting chance against harsh Mother Nature.

The wind whipped across the landscape, the grass as tall and lush as a field of ripened grain, swelling like waves all the way to the horizon. A few black eagles floated high up on the warm air currents, and the sky was such a seductive blue, it looked as if it could swallow up the earth. Every once in a while, Han Ma would dismount from his horse and snap his camera in an attempt to capture the magnificent scene unfolding before him.

Kelsang had spent the last few days tied up inside the schoolyard to prevent him from fighting with the dogs in town. Now that he was free, he was eager to find playmates. It didn't take him long to discover two strange little lemmings crouching with their paws to their chests in front of a small burrow. He was still some yards away and watched as they screeched and chirruped and threw up dust with their hind legs before darting down the hole. They reminded him of the marmots back home. Not long after he started digging into their hole, however, he looked up to find that Han Ma had already ridden off into the distance. So he gave up on this easy prey and went after his master.

An eagle landed on the grass up ahead, and Kelsang ran toward it, barking. But just as he was about to pounce, it slowly unfurled its large wings and started to flap, lifting into the sky like a flying carpet. Kelsang was starting to look rather naïve and inexperienced.

It was midday before he finally had a chance to show his credentials as the fine shepherd dog that he was. He and Han Ma drew up to a camp of three yurts and a crowd of herders who were covered in grasses from head to toe. They had spent the morning gathering hay for the winter and were now lying around in a leisurely fashion after their meal.

They were a courteous bunch. Each one went up to Han Ma in turn to welcome him. One of the young men asked his friend who this man was — riding a horse wearing city shoes.

"He's the teacher come from Harbin. What's-his-name who drives the Long Flag brought him here a few days ago."

"I mean how come he's riding without boots?" the young man said. "He looks like he's never ridden a horse before."

"Don't you recognize the horse he's riding? It's Hala.

He's as gentle as a cat. No one would lend a difficult horse to a teacher from the city."

"Haven't you ever thought of doing that?"

"Have you?"

"I don't know."

As the men continued their conversation, Kelsang lay down beside the horse, who was chewing on the grass. Up on the plateau, shepherd dogs weren't allowed inside yurts, and he stuck by this rule he'd learned as a puppy. These yurts may have been made from sheep's wool instead of yaks', but for Kelsang the principle was the same.

Besides the herdsmen, there were two shepherd dogs in the camp, and they were keeping a close eye on Kelsang. Although they hadn't shown him the courtesy that the young men showed Han Ma, they weren't looking for trouble, either. They could tell the huge dog was from the grasslands.

Milk was in abundance around this time of year, and the two dogs were fed plenty of meat, so they were stout, and each sported as glossy a coat as you could find anywhere. They were like the sheep they guarded, with nothing to do all day but eat.

With so many men on hand to help with the harvest, the two dogs must have been tired of new faces. When Han Ma and Kelsang arrived, they managed just a couple of symbolic barks from where they lay slumped in a corner, basking in the sun.

But everything changed when the men went inside, and the dogs, who were probably feeling bored, began to make trouble. They sauntered over to where Kelsang was dozing in the horse's shadow, still exhausted from his trip across the grasslands. The first to approach was the black dog, who was nowhere near as big as Kelsang but was unusually sturdy. Its left ear was torn, a war wound it wore with pride. As the dog got closer, it discovered that Kelsang wasn't like other dogs. He didn't jump to his feet to prepare for a fight, but stayed just where he was and continued to doze.

The dog circled Kelsang and stopped behind him. This was the perfect position. If it wanted, all it had to do was turn slightly, and it would be able to plant its teeth in Kelsang's ribs. It had used this method a few times before on intruding dogs, and each one had responded in exactly the same way — squealing, jumping up and flinging itself forward some five yards, then squeezing its eyes shut and howling. This gave the dog time to dart away and pretend to be tending the sheep, so that only the injured dog got a telling off for having disturbed the men inside.

But today's attack didn't go as planned. The black shepherd dog wasn't any slower than usual, and Kelsang stayed still right up until the last moment. In fact, the shepherd dog was thinking that Kelsang was a bit slow, and slow dogs have no place on the grasslands.

Before the shepherd dog could understand what was happening, a veil of darkness fell over its eyes, and its remaining ear felt as if it had been seared by a red-hot iron rod. It had experienced this feeling before as a young puppy when it had sniffed at a branding iron about to be used on its master's flock. The dog instantly forgot its plan of attack and tried to scramble away, screaming in pain.

The commotion brought the men outside, where they discovered Kelsang surrounded by two infuriated dogs. The black dog had lost its remaining ear, which from an aesthetic point of view was a pleasing outcome, making it look more symmetrical. The other dog was also the proud owner of a large wound, which ran down half its face. Spittle flew from their mouths as they barked at Kelsang, but he didn't seem to see them. He looked up sleepily at a shocked Han Ma standing among the herders.

"This dog is from Tibet. I wasn't going to bring him, but he won't leave my side. I'll tie him up. If we're not careful, he'll end up killing your dogs."

Han Ma signaled to Kelsang, who instantly sauntered over to his master and dropped to the ground with a thud. He glanced at the two dogs as if nothing had happened.

The oldest herder didn't seem to care that Kelsang had attacked his dogs, but the idea that Kelsang could kill his dogs did seem to offend him.

"Let him go, and let's see what he can do. I don't believe he can beat two dogs from Hulun Buir," he puffed, looking over at Kelsang. If Kelsang had been his dog, the old man would have let him feel his whip.

But Han Ma didn't want to let Kelsang go — the other two dogs had suffered enough — and it would probably only take seconds for the mastiff to knock them to the ground and rip their throats open. Then the situation would be even more difficult to resolve. One shepherd dog on the grasslands is like half a shepherd, and even though a fight would be a chance for Han Ma to show off what Kelsang could do, he wasn't going to allow it to happen.

The other men stood around cracking jokes and spurring the two men on. They were obviously hankering for some entertainment after a hard morning's work. The old man's face turned crimson as he insisted that Han Ma should let Kelsang go.

Kelsang was growing nervous, and he stood up a few times. He didn't like the way the old man was raising his voice and glaring at Han Ma. He stared fixedly at him, growling threateningly. Han Ma kept patting Kelsang on the head, encouraging him to lie back down.

During this confusion, a wolf appeared on the hill behind the camp. It was destined to be the sacrifice necessary to bring the argument to an end.

The men shielded their eyes from the dazzling sun and looked up at the black silhouette, like a paper cutout on the horizon. The two shepherd dogs now had a new enemy and a way to regain some lost face, but before they could get very far, the old man called them. They scuttled back and hid in the shadow of a horse cart.

Han Ma could see that the men looked worried. The old man had seemingly forgotten their argument and was swearing under his breath.

It only took a matter of moments before Han Ma realized what was going on. A sheep was tied up to another cart behind one of the yurts. It had lost all its wooly fleece down one side, revealing the soft, red flesh underneath. A few flies landed on it, drawn by the smell, and the sheep closed its eyes and twitched in pain.

"The same wolf that was here two days ago," one of the herders said, pointing to the animal pacing in the distance.

"Why don't you catch it?" Han Ma asked.

"We tried, but by the time our horses caught up with it, it had disappeared into the willows by the river. They're too dense to go tramping through. Dogs can manage it, but who knows how many wolves are hiding in there. The first dog that went in didn't come back out. We've tried three times to catch that wolf and lost two sheep. Now it stalks the camp during the day, showing off. I mean, what kind of behavior is that? I think we'll have to wait until the snow comes to do anything about it."

"My dog can get it," Han Ma said, without thinking.

"Then let him go for it," the old man said, overhearing the conversation. He pulled a beautifully decorated Mongolian knife from his waistband and continued, "If he doesn't manage it, you can leave him here."

Han Ma honestly didn't know if Kelsang would be able to catch the wolf, but he certainly didn't want to leave him out here on the grasslands. And if Kelsang did manage it, he might be able to patch up the argument.

Han Ma leaned down, embraced Kelsang and stroked

his long fur. The herders watched in surprise as the sleepy dog's muscles suddenly tightened, quivering ever so slightly. Summoning his strength, Kelsang let out a low growl like thunder.

He was waiting.

"Go," Han Ma urged him, pointing in the direction of the hillside.

Kelsang didn't set off at full speed, choosing instead to approach at a trot. The men burst into laughter. As soon as the wolf spotted Kelsang breaking away from the camp, it stopped pacing and watched as he drew closer.

Kelsang was excited to have received Han Ma's order. It had been two years since he had last chased a wolf, but he still knew what he was doing. He wasn't going to run at full speed. At this distance, there was every possibility that the wolf could escape, so he wouldn't waste too much energy in his approach. As he slowed down, his experiences on the grasslands came flooding back.

The wolf had let down its guard. After the herders' unsuccessful attempts to catch it, it no longer felt the need to run away. The wolf's arrogance allowed Kelsang to cover two-thirds of the distance between them before it finally realized it was in danger and started running for the willows, the best hiding place for miles around. The dog chasing it today was no ordinary dog. It didn't bark madly like the others had, but just followed him closely, silently. The wolf was scared, and its fear was like a black flame burning at its tail as the heavy sound of Kelsang's steps drew closer.

Kelsang noticed that this wolf was a different color than the ones on the Tibetan plateau. It was more like the color of dying autumn grass, sprinkled with salt and pepper. His nose twitched at its stench — that was certainly the same as on the plateau. This was a wolf, and wolves had always been and would always be his sworn enemies. Of that he was sure ever since he was a pup.

The willow grove appeared up ahead. Kelsang knew that if he let the wolf run into the trees, it would be like trying to chase it through a maze. He was close enough to attack now, so he gathered his strength and leapt forward, just as he had done so many times before. He sank his teeth into the wolf's backside. A crisp cracking sound followed, and one of the wolf's delicate hind legs broke in two.

The wolf twisted around in pain and tried to bite back, but Kelsang had already cast himself to the side. The wolf's bite met the air, and the force of its attempt sent it careering off balance. Rather than aiming straight for the wolf's neck, Kelsang ran around in front of it to block its escape into the willows.

Having nowhere to go, and realizing that this was probably going to be its last chance, the wolf unleashed all of its aggression. Dragging its broken leg, it charged straight at Kelsang. It had beaten many a shepherd dog using this method. They would lose their balance in an attempt to dodge it, leaving their necks open to a counter attack.

But Kelsang stood firm, and the wolf went crashing into his shoulder. It was like smashing headfirst into rock, and as the wolf slipped, Kelsang bit one of its front legs.

The wolf spun to a standstill, howling. There was barely any fight left in it. This time Kelsang went straight for its throat. As he bit into it, he discovered just how much smaller the wolves were here than on the plateau. Perhaps it was because these grasslands were far richer in food. Only the cruelest environments can produce truly strong animals.

The wolf was dead. Kelsang picked it up in his mouth as if it were a kitten and slowly jogged back to the camp, placing it at Han Ma's feet. Then he lay down.

Without a word, the old man threw his knife to Han Ma.

"He's not of this world," he said, giving a thumbs up.

The herders whistled as they threw their sickles over their shoulders and made for the grasslands, leaving Han Ma and Kelsang behind in the camp.

Kelsang was all anyone talked about for the rest of that sultry afternoon.

Once the school term started, Kelsang began to feel lonely. The local children were used to shepherd dogs and didn't give him a second glance. He was no longer special the way he had been at the School for Deaf and Blind Children. Furthermore, Han Ma was busy — the students were his primary focus. But Kelsang didn't think about all this too much. As long as he could be with Han Ma, that was enough for him.

Every morning, when Han Ma came out of his room carrying a bucket, Kelsang would be waiting for him, and together they would walk to the well to fetch water. While Han Ma was teaching, Kelsang would roam the schoolyard on his own. The local town dogs weren't like the dogs out on the grasslands. After only a couple of encounters, they concluded that Kelsang was not to be messed with and were careful to keep their distance.

When he was particularly bored, Kelsang would venture out into the grasslands on his own, but he always avoided camps for fear of encountering any more shepherd dogs. He would run on the soft, spongy grass, chasing small animals such as hares, field rats and larks. Then he would choose a patch of high ground and sleep, surrounded by the sweet fragrance of grass toasting in the sun. It would be dusk before he awoke, and by that time the smoke was rising from the chimneys in town. The children were already on their way home from school, scattering in all directions like small birds.

When he heard Han Ma calling his name, Kelsang would freeze for a moment before galloping off in the direction of the school, across the grass painted gold by the setting sun. Nothing in the world was more important than Han Ma's call. It was everything to him.

Kelsang repeated this routine every day.

But winter was arriving on the grasslands. The rain had been plentiful that summer, the grass lush, and the rodents — especially the rats and rabbits — had multiplied almost beyond control. If all these rodents were to make it to adulthood, it would spell disaster for the eco-system. They would munch their way through the grass and turn it into a barren wasteland. But the food chain works hard to keep its delicate balance. These rodents' predators also experienced a population explosion that summer. The sky was crowded with eagles, and the dirt roads were peppered with the corpses of weasels, crushed by vehicles traveling at night.

The Hulun Buir grasslands is one of the few places in China that still has wolves, and where they exist they are the kings of the food chain. Lush grass and ample prey worked wonders for the wolves, too. The wolf that had been harassing the old man's camp and eventually lost its life in Kelsang's jaws was probably just a warning of what was to come.

But there was one blessing in having so much food around for the wolves — they rarely attacked the sheep. The herdsmen consequently dropped their guard, and it was only when two young men from the city had a disastrous encounter with these animals that people realized just how many more wolves there were that year.

The young men's motorbike had broken down at the worst possible time, just as it was getting dark. But the two office workers, who were sick of wearing suits and were looking for some fun, didn't see it like that. As far as they were concerned, it would get light again soon. Someone was bound to come along who could give them a ride back toward home. And their bag of mushrooms, of course — they had been mushroom picking.

They had sleeping bags and a tent, and should be more than up to fending off the autumnal night, or at least so they thought. But as night fell, their face-off with the wolves began. Before long, a deep wail came floating through the darkness, getting progressively higher in pitch.

The two men huddled in their tent, screaming and banging together whatever they could find like crazed sports fans. But the phosphorescent dots of light slowly crept closer. The only thing that could stop them was fire.

They set alight their sleeping bags, tent, bags, hats, clothes, even the gas left in the motorbike tank in an attempt to keep the wolves at bay.

As the sun began to rise, three trucks carrying milk to Qili drove past, and the drivers spotted two naked, singed men running across the grasslands. The wolves had given up the fight and had slunk away.

From that day on, Han Ma refused to let the four children who lived out on the grasslands go home on their own. He started walking the mile and a half with them himself, but after a week, Kelsang took over. Every day, when school was let out, Kelsang would lead the children out the gates and across the grasslands to their camp before returning home on his own. It was like going back to his shepherding days. He was taking his four little sheep from one pen to another. He knew this job, and he was good at it.

The herders already knew all about this large black

dog and his performance at the old man's camp. The story had gone through the usual process of exaggeration, and by the time it reached them, Kelsang had bitten the wolf in half in one snap. They didn't doubt it for a moment after seeing him and always gave him bones and bits of cheese to gnaw on.

That winter was exceptionally cold. But it was Kelsang's fourth winter, and he wasn't bothered by the seasonal freeze. His internal body clock made its usual adjustments, and he quickly shed his summer coat in favor of his denser winter outfit. It was so thick that from a distance you could mistake him for a bear. As the temperature began to drop, Kelsang sensed that this winter was by no means going to be kinder than the long ones up on the plateau.

One early morning in November, as Kelsang emerged from his nest tucked under Han Ma's window, he saw that the grasslands were covered by a thick blanket of snow. The red ball of the morning sun looked as if it had been frozen to the horizon, unwilling to tear itself away from the silvery line across the landscape. The pure turquoise sky was completely still. It was as if the entire earth had frozen solid.

The herdsmen had already rounded up their horses to go out to pasture, but the horses didn't look as if they had entirely woken up. They trudged out into the fresh snow, their heads hanging as they walked toward the large well on the west side of town. Their white breath appeared almost solid in the cold air, and seemed to hang suspended, swallowing the horses up in a fog of their own breath.

Kelsang nuzzled into the snow and sneezed. It had been so long since his nose had been this irritated by the cold, but he was happy and went bounding off into the white meadow. He ran up to the newest camp on the outskirts of town. Two shepherd dogs watched as he ran toward them before he turned suddenly and galloped off in another direction, leaving them behind.

All of a sudden, Kelsang heard something. He stopped dead and listened. Then, retracing his tracks, he bounded back toward town.

Kelsang arrived just in time. Han Ma was opening the door when Kelsang careered into the yard. He only managed to take one step outside before Kelsang had flown around behind him, placed his front paws on his lower back and pushed him into the snow.

What followed could only be called a battle of wills as Han Ma hurled a freshly packed snowball at Kelsang, striking him on the nose and sending snow flying in every direction. Surprised and angry, Kelsang barked and pounced on Han Ma, dodging two more snowballs. Using all his might, he pressed Han Ma to the ground, a heavy paw against his chest, and within a flash, Han Ma's throat — shaking with laughter — was nestled in Kelsang's jaws.

Han Ma clung to Kelsang's neck.

The herdsmen, dressed in thick Mongolian robes and

dragging their herding sticks behind them, rode toward the pair. They could only shake their heads at the sight of the dog and teacher rolling around in the snow. They were just like children. How could a teacher play around like this, wearing only a woolen sweater in the Mongolian winter?

Of course, they knew how popular Han Ma was with the children. Even though he had arrived just three months before, the children were already starting to worry about what they would do when the school year came to an end.

This was only the first snow of winter. That year's terrible snowstorm came one afternoon at the end of December. Not even the most experienced of the old herdsmen had felt the change in the weather that day. There was nothing unusual in the sky. In fact, it was clear and bright, with the occasional eagle spreading its wings, floating on the warm air currents. Everything was tranquil, and it was fairly warm for a winter's day.

Many of the herders had driven their flocks out to faraway pastures in pursuit of sunny mountain slopes, where the wind whipped the tiniest snowflakes and the sheep could kick away the snow to find the grass beneath. But under this deceptively peaceful surface, disaster was waiting, and it was all the more frightening because of how suddenly it came.

That morning Kelsang felt something stir deep within him, a sign that something was about to happen. It was a completely different feeling from the one he had had out on the road near the guesthouse. It had none of the pressing urgency. The other shepherd dogs should have felt it, too, but they were already too domesticated. Kelsang was probably more closely related to their wild ancestors than they were themselves.

The other shepherd dogs only felt a bit fatigued that day, but as soon as their masters called, they jumped up and followed them out into the depths of the snow-covered pastures. No one wanted to pass on such a fine day. At the very least, it would be unwise to allow the flock to eat up the stock of hay so early in the winter. Something about the cold weather seemed to leave the sheep permanently unsatisfied.

That morning Kelsang didn't play his game with Han Ma, even though it had become somewhat of a routine. Han Ma hadn't noticed that anything was different. He had been busy all morning tending to the school's furnace. The dried cow dung had been soaked by the melting snow the previous afternoon, and now he couldn't get it to light. Eventually, he gave up and doused it with kerosene. The first children would be arriving soon, and he needed to get the heat going so that the classrooms would be toasty warm before lessons started. The weather was getting colder. Yang Yan had been kind enough to send a supply of cream against frostbite, and Han Ma had already passed it on to some of his pupils.

Even the slightest change in atmospheric pressure was enough to make Kelsang uncomfortable, but he didn't understand where this scary feeling was coming from. He had no way of finding out, either, no way of knowing where or when the disaster would begin. He was steadfast about one thing, though. No matter what, he wouldn't leave Han Ma today. He lay outside the classroom, the sound of his master's sonorous voice and those of the children reading out load floating through the wooden door. These sounds made him feel safe.

After the lunch bell, Kelsang went into the classroom and lay down at Han Ma's feet. The children finished their bowls of steaming meat congee, which had been cooking on the stove, and now they surrounded Han Ma. He had brought out his photo album and was opening up a whole new world to them. This had recently become an absolutely necessary post-lunch ritual.

A few bones were dropped onto the floor for Kelsang. Lying in the warm classroom at Han Ma's feet, he began to feel more satisfied. He drifted off to sleep, and his unease seemed to melt away in the warmth of slumber. It was already past two when he was awakened by Han Ma's calls. There was only one lesson in the afternoon during the winter because it grew dark so early. The four children who lived out on the grasslands were already waiting in the doorway, dressed in their fur-lined robes, fur hats and felt boots like tightly wrapped rice dumplings.

Suddenly an uneasiness grabbed hold of Kelsang again. It was time for him to go to work, to take the four children back to their homes. He paced around Han Ma slowly, unwilling to leave the classroom. He trusted this feeling. Experience told him to trust it. It wouldn't be wise to leave Han Ma right now, but he knew that protecting these children was what made his master happy. They were Han Ma's flock, and it was up to him to make sure that they didn't get lost in a snowstorm or attacked by a wolf.

And so Kelsang had no choice. He reluctantly followed the impatient children as they left the school. Usually, he led the way, making sure he didn't get too far ahead and only rushing back to the children if he sensed danger. Han Ma was shoveling snow in the yard as they left. Kelsang kept turning to make sure that he wasn't about to leave before running back to the noisy children.

As soon as they reached the path trodden through the snow, Kelsang tried to hurry the children along. That way he would be able to rush back to Han Ma sooner. Something was telling him that this was urgent, and he trusted his instincts completely. But things weren't going his way. The children were in no hurry and kept stopping to play in the snow. They ran around pulling off their hats and throwing them at each other, exposing their steamy heads to the cold air. Kelsang didn't know what to do.

The disaster announced itself in the form of a peculiar smell, or perhaps it was a sound coming from the depths of the earth. Instinct was telling Kelsang that it was building momentum. He ran in circles around the boisterous children, desperate to deliver them home and get back to Han Ma.

Kelsang blocked one child as he attempted to run out

into the grasslands, but the boy thought Kelsang wanted to join their game and threw his arms out as if to hug him, shouting in delight. The boy's arms missed, and like a penguin returning from the sea with a belly full of fish, he tumbled into the snow. Kelsang growled impatiently, and the boy looked up. He had grown up on the grasslands and had been babysat by shepherd dogs before. This was the sound they usually made if you pulled their fur or poked them in the eye by mistake.

The boy shuffled back a few paces in the snow, but the ferocious look in Kelsang's eyes disappeared as quickly as it had come, so he stumbled to his feet and went to stand with the other children. They were watching Kelsang nervously, no doubt recalling that this dog had bitten a wolf to death.

Kelsang could sense the children's fear, but there was nothing he could do. He started trotting in the direction of their homes, turning to look at them intently, hoping they would follow. But they didn't move. Kelsang ran back and bit hold of the corner of one boy's robe and started pulling at him, but the boy tried to shake him off.

The sudden change in Kelsang's attitude did have one good outcome, at least. The children stopped running and larking around. After a short while, they slowly began to walk again.

They were halfway home when the disaster finally struck. Kelsang heard a noise like the thunder of horses' hooves coming from the horizon. He let go of the boy's robe. The noise was buzzing in his eardrums. Dark clouds seeped into the white of the snow like a bottle of ink being poured into water and began to swirl toward them with frightening speed, like startled galloping horses.

Kelsang began to bark in fright. Instinct told him to take the children back to Han Ma since they were still probably closer to the school than to their homes. But the children hadn't yet grasped the gravity of the situation, and as Kelsang tried to steer them back, they stubbornly continued walking forward.

The wind was up, and huge snowflakes were swirling from the sky, which was already growing black, as if a giant dark curtain was being pulled across it. Try as he might, Kelsang couldn't get the children to change their minds. Now all he wanted was to get them in front of the stove as fast as possible, before the snow covered their way back.

Within a minute, the sky had gone completely black, the wind whistled around them, and visibility was reduced to less than five yards. Kelsang pushed on, trying to make out the path ahead. The children were silent. The one in front held tightly to his tail. Together, they trudged through the snow against the wind. Kelsang could barely smell a thing, and he was practically blind in the dark and swirling snow. He could only rely on his ability to judge its softness beneath his paws, and in this way, he slowly managed to stay on the more compact snow of the path.

Before long, Kelsang's heart-shaped mane had frozen, and he shook it, trying to break off the clumps of ice. But this small movement confused him and ended up sending him off the path. By the time he realized what had happened, he had no way of knowing how far back he had started straying. But worst of all, he suddenly realized that the last child was nowhere to be seen.

When the snow arrived, none of the herders thought at first that it was the beginning of a catastrophe. They had been lucky enough to bring their flocks in before it got too dark. At worst, the sheep were covered in clumps of ice, making them look like slowly moving hills as they drifted into their pens. The men didn't bother to brush the snow off themselves before slipping behind the felt doors of their yurts.

"The grasslands haven't seen a storm like this in a hundred years!" they gasped as they sipped bowls of burning-hot butter tea.

A steely look flashed across the dried-up wells of the old herdsman's eyes, and a strength seemed to rise up in him, the likes of which he hadn't felt since the day he managed to break in a beautiful foal many years before. He clasped at the collarbone he had broken after being thrown from the horse.

"The snowstorm thirty years ago wasn't as bad as this, and we lost many horses that night. They were frightened, and the head horse ran straight into the lake. I only just managed to stop the rest of my herd before they went crazy, too. I lost the fewest! And this is my souvenir," the old man said, raising his right hand, which was missing two fingers. "Who knows how many men were buried by the snow trying to save their horses. When the weather cleared the next day, we began finding them. They had taken off their clothes and died as if they were warming themselves by a fire. They froze to death like that," he mumbled, his toothless mouth twisting as he relived days gone by. "Why did they all die like that, as if they were crouching by the fire? All these years, I've wondered. Can you tell me why?" He looked up expectantly at the young herdsmen, but they were exhausted and had already drifted off to sleep.

So what happened that night? Countless sheep were swallowed up by the snow, as were many oxen, with only their black horns poking up through the drifts. Herds of horses huddled together, having no other shelter. When the storm finally let up, they were still there, standing in exactly the same spot, but life had left them during the coldest, darkest hours of the night. They continued standing there until spring, when they eventually thawed and fell to the ground.

It had been many years since the grasslands had seen a storm like this.

Kelsang started digging frantically into the slope, his back to the wind. He was like a mother fox trying to build a new burrow for her young. He nudged the three children into the hole, looked around to get his bearings and then ran out into the howling wind and snow.

He had to find the lost child.

Try as he might, Kelsang couldn't find the path. The traces of their footprints had been buried by fresh snow, and he had only his instincts to guide him. But despite the swirling flakes, he didn't lose his way.

By the grace of the creator of all living things, his coat this winter was thicker than ever before, as if somehow in anticipation of the storm. The biting cold wasn't painful, but the wind did make it hard for him to breathe. He pushed ahead with each step, fighting against the soft snow, his nose pressed close to it as it was whipped up by the wind. Where was the scent of that child? In this weather it would be impossible to pick up.

Kelsang walked and walked. He felt like he was covering twice the distance he had done with the children. But he wouldn't stop until he found a whiff of the boy's scent frozen on the snow. He would cover hundreds of square yards if necessary.

All of a sudden, he felt something underfoot, despite the icy clumps frozen to his paws. Crazed, he ran in circles, scrapping at the deep drifts until he uncovered the rounded shape of a child crouched in the snow with his hands over his face.

He was still alive.

He had tripped and fallen. By the time he had managed to scramble to his feet, his friends had disappeared into the white-gray of the snowstorm. His shouts had been broken into fragments by the wind, only to fall around him. Dropping to the ground, the child had covered his face, curled himself into a ball and drifted into a confused sleep. If Kelsang hadn't found him when he did, he likely would have been buried more deeply, never to wake up again.

The boy remained huddled in a ball, even after Kelsang dug him out. Kelsang tugged at the mittens covering his face and licked his cheeks with his hot tongue. It took another ten minutes before the boy could get to his feet and begin to follow Kelsang. He didn't know where the dog was taking him, or where his friends were, but at least he was no longer on his own.

Kelsang found his way back to the other children without any problems, and within half an hour, he had dug them out of the burrow. They were huddled inside like startled quails and were soon covered by a fresh blanket of snow. Kelsang gently brushed the new snow away and then began digging another hideout where he stored all four of them. He then lay down at the entrance, blocking the galloping snow.

He had done the right thing. Had he taken the other three children to look for the missing boy, they would have collapsed, one by one, from exhaustion, and Kelsang would have been helpless. They would have all perished — there could be no doubt about it. No one had taught him to dig a hole on a slope facing away from the wind and to hide children inside, nor did experience tell him to do so. He had never been in a storm like this before, not even on the Tibetan plateau. It was all instinct. Instinct told him how to act in the face of nature's cruelty.

It had been a tiring few hours. Once the children settled, Kelsang, too, collapsed with exhaustion, tucking his nose into his belly and drifting off to sleep. A long, disturbing dream followed. He was a puppy chasing his mother's shadow. In fact, as far as he could remember, his mother had only ever been a shadow, whose warmth he had never felt since. Then he was tied up, and all he could think about was trying to bite the man with the dark cheeks. His laugh scraped across Kelsang's eardrums like shards of glass being shaken in a bottle. But nothing was more frightening than the vision of Han Ma walking away, leaving him because he had lost the four little children. Kelsang was running after him, but no matter how hard or fast he ran, there was an insurmountable distance between them. He gave up, crying out in despair, and watched Han Ma disappear over the horizon.

Kelsang woke with a yelp, like a little puppy. He jumped to his feet and shook the snow from his fur. It was dark. With horror, he realized that his dream was becoming a reality — the four children were nowhere to be seen. He barked in alarm and bucked until he bumped against something solid beneath the snow. A fresh snowfall had covered the four children while he had been sleeping, that was all. After brushing the snow away, he carefully pulled them apart and began licking their cold faces until they wriggled awake and opened their eyes.

The wind had yet to abate, but Kelsang pulled at the children's clothes, urging them to stand up. After a few attempts, he gave up in disappointment. They no longer had any energy, and he understood that there was no way he could make them go on. He didn't know what to do. Instinct was telling him to stay and keep watch over them and to just keep barking. This was what he had done out on the grasslands when one of the sheep was injured and unable to move. This was how he got his master's attention.

He lowered his larynx and started to bark, but the sound didn't travel far, and before long he began to doubt this strategy. Whatever happened, he couldn't leave these children. He kept circling them, stopping every now and again to look out into the distance.

"Go find Mr. Han Ma. Find Mr. Han Ma, dog," one of the children said, shivering.

This was a clever child. If he had told Kelsang to find one of the herdsmen, he wouldn't have recognized the name. But to Kelsang, the sound of "Han Ma" was the most important one on earth. He stared at the children huddled together.

"Go find our teacher. Find Mr. Han Ma. Go!" The child pointed to where Kelsang kept looking, thinking it must be the direction of the school.

Kelsang understood, and now he had to make a difficult choice. He knew he would be going against Han Ma's strictest instructions. He was to take the children back to their camp and was certainly not to leave them. It's extremely difficult for a dog to make this kind of decision. But it seemed impossible to carry out his task now anyway, and perhaps it would be better to find Han Ma, who could then tell him what to do.

Kelsang brushed the snow off the children one last time and then ran out into the night. He kept sinking into the deep snow as he ran, although his paws never touched the solid ground beneath. All he could do was leap like a deer, which turned out to be incredibly tiring.

No road. No tracks. Kelsang kept stopping to try to figure out the way.

One and a half hours later, the herdsmen and Han Ma were in the school discussing what to do next when Han Ma heard Kelsang's bark. It wasn't particularly loud, but it was getting closer, the sound somehow fighting its way through the heavy wind and snow. The herdsmen were exhausted after riding around half the night in search of the children, but the sound energized them, and they crowded into the doorway looking out into the darkness.

Covered in snow, Kelsang crashed through them and ran straight to Han Ma, barking himself hoarse. He had hardly ever barked like this, but before his master could reach out to touch him, he turned and ran to the door. He stopped and looked back at Han Ma.

"What are we waiting for? He wants to take us to the children!" the old man shouted, pulling on his fur hat. His grandson was among them.

And so they mounted their horses and went out into the depths of the storm under the leadership of the black mastiff.

The four children drifted off to sleep, tucked up under heavy animal skins in the warmth of the yurt. They would have to wait until tomorrow to tell their classmates about their frightening ordeal. None of the herdsmen felt like sleeping, and instead they pottered around in the yurt all night. The older ones recalled the last snowstorm — the cows frozen like lumps of stone, the felt as brittle as paper, and the black stallion who was born that night and had gone on to win first prize at the Naadam Fair.

They drank until their cheeks were flushed, and then the old man suggested they go out to take a look at the miraculous dog. By the time they shuffled outside, the snow had almost stopped, and only the tiniest flakes were falling from the dawn sky.

Despite being covered by a thick layer of snow and ice, Kelsang seemed impervious to the cold. But when he saw Han Ma, he jumped to his feet and shook himself off.

Such a magnificent dog, such beautiful long black fur shining a metallic blue in the dawn light. He was as sturdy as a bear, a full thirty-five inches tall, his legs as thick as tree trunks. He had a carefree look in his eyes as he sauntered toward Han Ma.

The herdsmen couldn't help but click their tongues in admiration.

Han Ma stroked Kelsang's head, just as he had done many times before, and then crouched down and put his arms around the mastiff's neck.

"Such a magical dog!" the old man gasped, lifting his

glass of rice wine as if about to make a toast and then pouring it over Kelsang.

He started singing an old Mongolian folk song in honor of the handsome horse who had won first prize at Naadam Fair, and the other herdsmen joined in, one by one.

It was a bleak but powerful tune, and it cut through the silver snow of the day's first light and echoed across the grasslands.

Afterword

THE VAST EXPANSE of the Hulun Buir grasslands.

If you ever have a chance to go there, walk deep into the grasslands. Just as you draw close to the camp that has been in the distance for some time, you'll be greeted by a crowd of large shepherd dogs barking loudly. Among these fierce dogs, you'll find a few whose barks are like thunder, whose tails are thick and curly, whose fur is so black it shines like a crow's wings.

Inside the yurts, the old herdsmen will tell you that among the dogs lying outside, the black ones are descended from a purebred Tibetan mastiff. A magnificent mastiff that once lived on these grasslands.

And, of course, if you go to the school in town, you'll be able to see the enormous black dog for yourself.